SOPHIE'S
FOR NO-V

By

Kingsley L. Dennis

Illustrated By

David M. Miller

BTB

SOPHIE'S SEARCH
FOR NO-WHERE

Published by Beautiful Traitor Books –
http://www.beautifultraitorbooks.com/

ISBN-13: 978-0-9954817-9-4 (paperback)

First published: June 2017

Front Cover Design: David M. Miller
Back Cover Design: Ibolya Kapta

The author wishes to give particular thanks to David M. Miller and Ibolya Kapta for their generous assistance and their willingness to bring this special project to life. The Imaginal World shall forever be…

From Kingsley L. Dennis

To all the *Young Dreamers*

~ for keeping the world alive ~

From David M. Miller

For my wife Anita, who was so encouraging and supportive; and for Max and Oliver - may you, too, find your way to the Imaginal World.

Kingsley L. Dennis, PhD, is an author and researcher. He currently lives in Andalusia, Spain.

He can be contacted at his personal website:
www.kingsleydennis.com

By the same author

The Seeker

The Custodians: A Play in 3 Acts

The Foundation: The Enigma of a Community

The Citadel: A Mystery at the Heart of Civilization

The Phoenix Generation: A New Era of Connection, Compassion, and Consciousness

Mundus Grundy: Trouble in Grundusland

Meeting Monroe: Conversations with a Man who Came to Earth

Dawn of the Akashic Age: New Consciousness, Quantum Resonance, and the Future of the World (co-authored with Ervin Laszlo)

Breaking the Spell: An Exploration of Human Perception

New Revolutions for a Small Planet

The Struggle for Your Mind: Conscious Evolution & The Battle to Control How We Think

The New Science & Spirituality Reader (co-edited with Ervin Laszlo)

New Consciousness for a New World

After the Car (co-authored with John Urry)

David M. Miller is a San Francisco native and lifelong resident of the Bay Area. He can be contacted at his personal website:
http://www.davidmillerart.com/

CHAPTERS

CHAPTER ONE – SOPHIE'S DREAM

In Dreams Begin Responsibilities…

There are dreams, and then there are *dreams*. And if you are one of the very few then maybe you have experienced those dreams that lay within dreams. This is a realm that is often more real than the one you experience upon waking up. And that was Sophie's dilemma – her dreams seemed more real than the everyday world. And that was why she began to suspect that the everyday world may not be the real thing, after all. And then it happened again…

…Sophie wandered another time down the corridors and halls of what was the most astonishing house. It was more like a palace than a house, so spectacular was its appearance. Each room Sophie looked into was decorated with the most extravagant furniture she had ever seen. Huge chairs with velvet upholstery and six legs looked as if they were waiting for giants to occupy them. The great house was ornate and extravagant, with golden curtains and hanging chandeliers that sparkled with rainbow reflections. Long corridors stretched away in many directions, seemingly without end. This was not the first time Sophie had been here. She had walked the halls and corridors of the same house over and over again for what must have been weeks now. Then again, time in such places never seems to go in straight lines. The idea of weeks was a reflection back to Sophie's time in her normal life. But here, in this house, things and time, and timely things, were just altogether different – somewhat like ice cream and mud cake.

Things were upside down too. Along the walls of some of the corridors were pictures and paintings hanging upside down. Landscapes and portraits showed inverted worlds and faces. Suns and stars appeared as if rising from below, whilst the earth above covered the cosmos like a terrestrial sky. So many times Sophie had wandered the corridors of this house; and each time exploring a little more… and each time not getting far enough. You see, there's that problem with time again! As she walked she felt the carpets soft beneath her feet, and she only realized when she looked down that she was barefoot. Where were her normal shoes? It all seemed so unreal at the same time that it felt some kind of normal. Was that what it felt like to have stepped into another world? Sophie stopped to listen to the silence. Not even the sound of a breeze or Nature's offerings could be heard through the magnificent open windows.

SOPHIE'S SEARCH
FOR NO-WHERE

Often the glare of the sun streaming in made it difficult for
Sophie to see everything clearly. This place, she thought to herself, is
not a part of *my* world. Treading softly, Sophie followed some steps
that went down at the end of one of the corridors. She found herself
once again in a place she remembered - a spectacular garden of the
brightest colors. She could see small bird-like creatures of four wings
that chirped in sweet squawks darting through the branches of trees.
This was the only sound to be heard, the bird-song of the strange
flying feathered creatures. Sophie felt that they were singing especially
to mark her arrival. And there, not far away through the trees, stood
the apparition of the tall shimmering lady. Sophie had seen this lady
several times yet had never managed to reach her or speak with her.
She slowly stepped towards the shining lady who stood elegantly
dressed in flowing white robes. As she approached, Sophie noticed that
the lady had the most penetrating gaze, firm yet soothing, and almost
golden hair.

Then the same thought occurred to Sophie, as it always did before. 'I
know I am in my dream again…I must not wake up… I must hold on.'
But you know how it is. Once such a thought enters into your mind, it

plants the seed of opposites. It's like someone telling you not to do something, so of course you go and do it anyway. If there was a law for this it would probably be called the law of contrary action. So, as soon as this thought occurred to her, Sophie knew she would lose her grip - as it always happened. Just a little longer! She pleaded…but already the world-more-real-than-the-real-world was slowly beginning to slip away from her. Each time Sophie had the realization that she was inside one of her own dreams then she would lose her dreaming concentration and the inevitable would happen - she would wake up. Yet she also noticed something else. At each attempt she would gain a little more time before her dream would dissolve around her. In these extra moments of lucid time Sophie would try to get closer to the shimmering lady. On this last occasion she stepped toward the apparition, reaching out to her, only to see her endearing smile change into a frown of disappointment. The house began to disappear into thousands of tiny filaments like falling snow until nothing was left. Sophie stood alone in the middle of complete whiteness as if suddenly engulfed by a blanketing fog.

'Damn it, not again!' said Sophie under her breath as she sat up in bed. The signs of early dawn had already crept under her curtains. As any good dreamer knows, these flickers of daylight always come to kick you out of bed. They are like tongues that lick you back into everyday reality. For Sophie, who had been dreaming of the house for so many weeks, she felt frustrated that she had still not managed to reach the shimmering lady – whoever she was! And yet Sophie also had a niggling feeling inside that the strange apparition was waiting for her. Sophie was a little angry with herself. She knew she had to make more effort – to dream harder. Yet Sophie was already a dreamer - too much of a dreamer according to her family and friends. She was often accused and teased for always being 'in another world,' or something to that effect. Sophie's mind often drifted into wild imaginings when she was in class, at home, or even when hanging out with her friends. It was as if, for Sophie, this world that everyone lived within could not hold her attention long enough. It wasn't that she was bored. She just felt that there were other worlds to be a part of too. And that was normal for Sophie. What was not normal was that other people around her didn't seem to question the world they walked around in. So, you can guess that Sophie was somewhat between…well, between two worlds – which you might think is not a bad thing. There are worse things to be between, such as between two hungry sharks, or between two bread buns in a giant hamburger factory. But that's another matter…

The house where Sophie lived in her regular world was much smaller than the mansion in her dreams. And the pictures and decorations on the walls were the right way up too. Well, the right way up for this world at least, thought Sophie. Then again, does it really matter if the pictures consist of a horse pulling a canal boat or three flying ducks? Really, what was the point!

As Sophie sat down for breakfast she noticed, as she always did, how everything was a routine. Her family – the Saunders family – were nothing if not regular in their ways. In fact, the Saunders were far too regular for Sophie's liking. Her younger brother, James, would eat his cereals with orange juice, and make faces at her. Her father, Richard, would eat his toast with a mug of tea whilst flicking through the morning news on his tablet. And her mother, Alice, would be fretting around the kitchen as if she was holding the world on her shoulders like Atlas. It would be the same almost every morning.

School was not much better either. In her classes Sophie stared at her teachers as they droned on like military drill sergeants, explaining one particular rule after another. Whether a grammar rule or a mathematical equation, everything seemingly had its ordered place. Sophie wrote all of this down dutifully in her notebooks, just as all the other students did. Yet the stuff never really went into her head. The equations, rules, laws, whatever they were called, all swam like ink eels across the lanes of her paper as if racing for some imaginary finish line. Sophie spent more time watching these eely-squiggle races than she did trying to juggle them in her head into concrete facts. Nobody knows what facts really are, Sophie would say to herself as she stirred the pot of squiggly-stew ink lines across her pages. What Sophie didn't know, or didn't care to know, was that facts were placed into the world in order to make it *seem* more real, even if it wasn't so. Now – that's a fact!

Between classes Sophie would wander the halls of her school imagining she was being taken on conveyor belts to every place. All she had to do was to keep her balance and not to fall over, and the moving conveyors would carry her to the next destination. Being at school for Sophie was like being in some factory for animated dolls and puppets, with each one having a battery pack somewhere inside them that powered their movements. Sophie would smile to herself, seeing certain classmates slowly wind themselves down before coming to a complete stop – battery dead. It only her battery would last long

enough in *the other world* to get her to reach the shimmering lady.

Small flowers were attempting to grow between the cracks in the

concrete pavement of the schoolyard. One day Sophie's friend, who

was called Jenny, had asked why it was that such flowers grew amongst

the concrete where there was no grass.

'Because they can,' Sophie had replied.

Back at home Sophie's mum, Alice, moved nervously through the

house searching in each of the rooms. You see, Alice was one of those

people who was always losing or misplacing things. It wasn't a lack in

memory, rather a weakness in location-attention (something the

medical profession has recently abbreviated to 'loca').

'Sophie, do you know where my reading glasses are?'

'No,' called back Sophie.

'Can you help me look for them?' Whenever something could not be

found in the house the usual thing was to ask Sophie. It was because

she had a knack of finding things that others couldn't find. For Sophie

it was really quite easy. She would close her eyes and imagine the object

and visualize it clearly. Then she would walk through the house with this image in her head. More often than not she would get a strange feeling in her stomach whenever she was near to the object. Finding it after that was as easy as mashing soft potato.

'Okay. Give me a minute.' Sophie finished what she was doing and then went to find her mum's glasses. Sophie, at eleven years old, was thin and slightly small for her age. Her auburn hair hung long down her shoulders, and cupped her slightly oval face. Sophie had pale skin, softened by a reddishness in her cheeks. She was smaller than most of the other girls in her school year - and certainly more delicate too. Sometimes her mother would jest that Sophie would make an excellent ballerina, if only she could focus her attention for long enough. Sophie would always smile back. She knew that she was already a ballerina, but not in the world where people like her mother lived.

...*Leaving* the steps behind, Sophie once again entered the exquisite garden where four-winged birds squawked and flew. And once more she saw the shimmering lady ahead of her through the trees. Sophie focused her attention upon the apparition and cleared her mind, as she had been practicing before. Slowly she drew closer and closer, all the time fixing her gaze upon the lady's face. When Sophie was only a few feet away the lady, who stood tall above Sophie's height, slanted her head to one side and smiled.

'Sophie, come here.' The voice seemed to ring out in a chime.

Sophie stepped even closer until she could almost touch the flowing fabric of the lady's robe. The lady bent down a little to put her face closer to Sophie's. Her long golden hair smelled of the essence of crushed springtime flowers.

'Sophie, you *must* enter…you have to dream harder.' The soft musical voice of the lady flowed into Sophie's ears like a river of warm honey. Sophie was stunned into silence.

'Sophie,' the lady said again, this time with a more urgent tone, 'there is little time…' Suddenly Sophie's concentration shattered into tiny fragments. Everything snapped as if a catapult had been sprung.

SOPHIE'S SEARCH
FOR NO-WHERE

SOPHIE'S SEARCH
FOR NO-WHERE

'NO!...' Sophie screamed as she bolted upright in her bed. Not again...

not again, she whimpered as her small hands clenched into whitened

balls of angst. She had been so close, so close...and yet. Yet that is

sometimes how things are. Maybe in the world of always-on television

and shopping we are used to getting what we want. But there are other

places, other realms, where a little something *extra* is

required...something that is beyond the push of a button.

Admittedly it was a drawback for Sophie. But Sophie being

Sophie – a quiet determined young girl (and we should never

underestimate the power of a quiet, determined young person), the

disappointment only made her more resolute to reach her goal.

'Another nightmare darling?' asked her mum over breakfast that

morning.

Sophie's father, Richard Saunders, raised an inquisitive eyebrow as he

quickly looked up from his tablet, and then continued flicking over the

screens.

'Yes, a waking nightmare,' mumbled Sophie under her breath.

Her younger brother, James, giggled and picked his nose. Sophie

thought that his freckled face must have been stolen from one of those cereal packets he constantly ate from. He was, she thought, the ideal poster kid for those pop-up-whatcha-thingies that dissolve in the mouth and help you get away with everything. Life in some ways could be like that – something that dissolved in the mouth and was gone before you even got a good taste of it.

But not for Sophie. She would not let things dissolve in her mouth so easily. She would try, and try again…and next time she would damn well succeed – or her name was not Sophie Saunders.

…There was a unique symmetry to the upside-down pictures in the large house. It was not a consistent or straight symmetry, and certainly not one with regular logic. Rather, there was a sense of a kind of irregular logic working in a non-obvious way. Well, it's one of those things that modern rational minds find hard to pick up on. Actually, being out of your 'right mind' is often the best way to pick up on such things. Sophie was beginning to *get it* now - each time she walked down the corridors she sensed something extra. It was as if her perspective was leaning into the pictures more and more, rather than the pictures coming out to meet her. In this way the topsy-turvy paintings began to make sense, as the person looking at them actually entered into

participation with the scene. When Sophie felt this she knew it didn't matter which way up - or down - the pictures were hung. You were only the right way up/down when you were actually inside the pictures themselves. On the outside there is no logic, no consistency - on the inside everything made sense. And it also helped Sophie to keep her focus. She knew this now. By merging her concentration with things and items in the house she was able to maintain her presence. The house was actually helping Sophie to maintain her attention as it guided her along. So that's the trick! realized Sophie - you had to be *with* the house - on its level - and not separate from it. Knowing this, Sophie could now easily make her way down the steps and into the florid and incandescent garden where the shimmering lady stood waiting.

'Sophie, this time you *must* enter...' The now familiar soft voice reached out to the young girl and grabbed her.

'Enter where?'

'The Imaginal World awaits you...you must dream into it.'

'The Imaginal World?' Sophie did not understand. 'Why?'

'If you do this one thing and nothing else, then your life will have been fulfilled. Yet if you do everything else in your life and fail to do this one thing, you shall have done nothing. You came here for the Imaginal World, and within it you must seek – you must *find!*

SOPHIE'S SEARCH
FOR NO-WHERE

'Find what? Where?'

'You must find your way to No-Where, in No-Place. If you *need* enough, and want little enough, then you shall find your way. Others like you have tried, and some are still trying. You may meet them upon your journey. Not everyone succeeds in reaching No-Where, or finding No-Place. It is not for everyone. For most people, no such place as No-Place exists. Are you ready for this journey?'

Sophie looked directly into the lady's eyes and nodded. 'Yes, I wish to seek and find No-Where.'

The shimmering lady turned and pointed to the far side of the garden. 'There, go and you shall find the Green Man. Without him you cannot enter through the door that takes you into the Imaginal World. You must grab onto his robe and refuse to let go until he grants you access. Go, now, before he leaves - you have little time. And Sophie, remember that everything is different over there. Trust in the one true place where your own questions lie.' The lady smiled gently as she once again bent her head down to look upon Sophie, before dissolving into speckled filaments of light dust.

SOPHIE'S SEARCH
FOR NO-WHERE

In the far corner of the garden Sophie saw movement, a figure flitting behind a yew tree. She walked quickly over to the far side of the garden, keeping her concentration, and heeding the lady's warning of there being little time. Sophie followed a path that wound between rows of bristling bushes with bright blue flowers, as butterfly-like creatures the size of small sparrows fluttered past her head. As she brushed past the branches of the yew tree she saw a figure all dressed in green walking away down a narrow path parallel to the garden wall. Quickening her steps she followed the figure, her heart beating faster inside her chest. She knew she could not lose her concentration now. Time was trying to creep in at the edges…she had to move fast. The Green Man had now reached a door in the garden wall and was reaching into his pockets. *I must keep focused, I must keep focused* repeated Sophie to herself as she saw that the figure was placing a key in the lock of a large wooden door. Just as he was about to turn the handle Sophie reached up to him and grabbed onto his green robe, exactly as the lady had told her to do.

The Green Man shot Sophie a sudden look which almost made her let go in surprise. Yet her little hand kept its firm grip upon the green robe – a strange green that seemed to reflect the garden around him. Small movements appeared to flicker across the robe the way tall grass wavers in a breeze. Sophie looked up into the man's face and saw that he had a darker complexion, and a well-cut black beard that seemed to frame his deep-set dark eyes. The Green Man did not move and remained still, staring deeply into Sophie's face making her feel like an uninvited trespasser.

'I need access to the Imaginal World,' said Sophie after what seemed like a long pause. The Green Man said nothing. 'You must grant me access,' said Sophie again, this time in a firmer voice.

The Green Man raised his eyebrows. 'Must I?' When he spoke, it was with a rich, smooth baritone voice that seemed to sing like the birds. Sophie hesitated. 'Or I will not let go!'

The Green Man looked down to where Sophie was grabbing hold of his robe, and he appeared to give a faint smile.

'Why do you wish to enter the Imaginal World?'

'To find No-Where, at No-Place,' replied Sophie. As soon as she said that she had the faint sensation that she was beginning to lose the grip on her concentration. The edges of the dream were beginning to fade. *I must not wake up now!* Sophie screamed to herself inside. As if knowing Sophie's state the Green Man fixed his eyes more deeply upon her, and Sophie immediately felt a renewed energy of focus and attention.

SOPHIE'S SEARCH
FOR NO-WHERE

'And what do you want with No-Where?' he asked.

Sophie paused, not sure of what exactly to say. Then, as if trusting in her instinct she replied, 'To know the answers to my questions. It's what I have to do.'

'Are you ready to search for what you yet do not know?'

'Yes,' replied Sophie, again with a firm voice.

'Answers don't mean anything unless you have the right questions. Do you have the right questions Sophie?' The Green Man's gaze seemed to penetrate right through Sophie, as if she too was just another dream image. She felt as if he could see into her every thought and feeling.

'I don't know,' she said honestly. 'All I know is that I need to do this. It is time.'

The Green Man nodded his head and with his right hand still upon the door handle, turned it and opened the large wooden door.

'In dreams begin responsibilities,' he said as he stepped through the door with Sophie following behind. Her hand was still grabbing tightly onto the Green Man's robe as she passed the threshold.

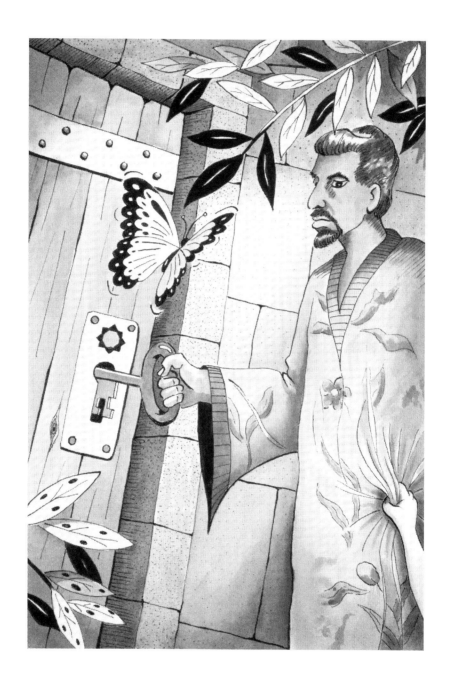

CHAPTER TWO - THE QUEST BEGINS

What do you want to slow down for - do you wish to delay your destiny?

The path before her resembled a dirt track, with wild, overgrown fields on either side. The cloudless sky was illuminated by some unknown source, as Sophie could see no sun above. Nor could she see any sign of the Green Man, and yet she had been holding onto his robe only a moment before. Sophie also realized that she didn't need to keep her concentration so focused all the time. She knew she was in no danger of waking up now that she was in…where was she? Ah yes, the shimmering lady had referred to it as the Imaginal World. Well, she was here now…no time for hanging around. As anyone who's dealt with time knows, as soon as you start thinking about it then it begins to do funny things, like speeding up or slowing down – or going bendy-like.

With just a tiny bit of trepidation Sophie set out on the track ahead of her, not knowing what to expect. As she looked down at the path she realized that she was still wearing her pajamas. She then felt a little foolish, and wished she had dressed properly for the quest. How was she to reach her destination wearing pajamas? No self-respecting adventurer would set-out for the road to No-Where in their pajamas. Sophie was a little mad with herself for being so unprepared. She had been so focused on her dreaming that she had neglected to think about the more practical things. As she was thinking this something dropped down from the sky in front of her. It was a small bird with bright yellow-red plumage. It lay on the track and appeared to twist and convulse before becoming stone still. Sophie bent down to inspect it. 'Oh, poor little bird,' she said as she cupped it in her hands. 'What happened to you?'

'You killed it,' said a voice from behind.

Sophie almost jumped in fright as she spun around. Behind her stood an old wizened man in tattered clothes and a long white beard that ran the length of his thin stomach.

'What? What do you mean I killed it? I didn't!' stammered Sophie.

'The bird was flying past as you were being angry with yourself and doing your self-pity routine. Pitiful! Your woe-is-me, look-at-me-in-my-pajamas anger killed that bird which did nothing to you except fly by at the wrong moment.'

Sophie's face dropped and a horrible sensation erupted in her stomach.

'Weren't you warned to be careful here? You Regulars think you can all be dreamers.' The old man made a large, loud sigh and shook his head.

'What do you mean, Regulars?'

'You folks from the Regular World. Now and again some of you come here, thinking you know everything. Yet your minds are an endless carnival of useless things - you have no idea how to use your thinking tools. You have no idea of your responsibilities – no wonder the Regular World is in the state it's in!' The old man grumbled to himself and huffed as he reached out his hand to Sophie. 'Give me the bird, young lady.' The old man took the bird and whispered something into its tiny bird ear. Almost immediately the bird sprang up into life, chirped a few notes of gratitude, and flew away.

'Oh, that's amazing! How did you do that?' said Sophie fascinated. The old man continued to mumble and grumble under his breath.

'How? How! You want to know how and yet you never ask why - typical of you Regulars!' The old man began to shuffle away.

'Okay…why?'

'Why? Why would you want to know, little miss Regular? You don't even know why you ask. Why? Pork pie, that's why!' The old man hobbled past Sophie and carried along down the track in the opposite direction. Sophie followed after him.

SOPHIE'S SEARCH
FOR NO-WHERE

'Do you know how I can find No-Where?'

'Where is No-Where?'

'It's in No-Place.'

'Mm, you want to find No-Where in No-Place…I suppose you'll be asking for No-thing next!'

Sophie lowered her eyes. 'No,' she said quietly, 'just No-Where. I really need to find it. Can you help me, please?'

'Maybe I can, maybe I can't.' The old man sniffed indignantly. 'Besides, you've only just got here. Why do you want to go No-Where so soon? Bored already are you, little miss Regular?'

'Look, my name's Sophie,' said Sophie with a tone of irritability in her voice.

'It doesn't matter what they call you over there. Names and words have different meanings here. You could be a Sophie over there but here you could be a Lucy.'

'Why would I want to be a Lucy?'

The old man shook his head. 'Peanuts and daffodils - what a blockhead you are, girl! I didn't say you would *want* to be a Lucy. I said you *could* be a Lucy. The difference is bigger than your two hands wide apart. Why don't you listen, girl?'

'And why don't you be more polite!' snapped back Sophie.

SOPHIE'S SEARCH
FOR NO-WHERE

The old man just chuckled to himself. 'Because I'm following my destiny, that's why. And what are you doing?'

'I'm trying to follow my destiny too,' said Sophie somewhat forcefully.

'And how do you know if it's your destiny or not?' asked the old man with a smirk.

'Well, I follow what feels right... how do you know if it's yours?'

'Because,' said the old man as he pulled out a scroll of paper from inside his ragged clothes, 'it is written here on the Scroll of Destiny. But you weren't to know that, of course, because you never thought to ask. Regulars with their regular thinking, puff!'

Sophie had to walk quite fast to keep up with the old man. The dry dirt track left the wild fields behind on both sides and gradually changed into a pleasant path that descended into a green, fertile valley. Light still shone in the sky, from somewhere, and the day was pleasantly warm - neither too cold nor too hot.

'It seems, young Regular, that you are walking with me. Well, better than against me I suppose!' The old man grinned at Sophie.

'Yes, I am walking with you. I'd like to share the road with you for a while, if you don't mind? And you can call me Sophie.'

'Whether I mind or not is beside the point since you have already taken the decision to do so without my asking. Yet if you come with me you must agree not to question what I do. You are still too regular to understand this world. Agreed?'

'Agreed!' Sophie said with a nod of her head.

'Good. And I know what I *can* call you. What I choose to call you is another matter. Since you are not a part of my destiny I can call you Lucy, and it won't have any consequences upon my future. How it will affect yours, little Lucy, I cannot say!' The old man began to whistle.

'Okay, Lucy is fine with me. Whatever! And do you have a name?' asked Sophie.

'Yes.' The old man kept on whistling. Sophie waited and waited.

'Well?' she asked finally.

'Well is for water. Look, didn't anyone ever teach you not to ask yes or no questions?'

'Okay, okay. So, would you please tell me your name?'

The old man scrunched his face as if thinking. 'Why, of course, it's Rumpelstiltskin.' The old man let out a loud cackle. 'Sorry, wrong story! Mm… I suppose you can call me Gabby. It will do,' he said as he let out a fart. Sophie giggled behind her hand, and Gabby continued to whistle.

SOPHIE'S SEARCH
FOR NO-WHERE

Sophie thought the old man looked so thin and fragile beneath his rags, and yet he walked with a strong healthy pace that was difficult for her to keep up with. The old man Gabby appeared full of vigor despite his appearance. Sophie now paid more attention to her surroundings, not really sure how far she had walked since first arriving. She noticed that the sunlight was a lesser brightness, and that there was no wind or breeze. The valley rose up high on either side of her and stretched as far into the distance as she could see. Looking more closely at the trees in the valley she noticed that they varied in so many different shades of green. This was surely not like the trees back home. Here the different shades were so noticeable, like on a painter's palette.

'Gabby, you're walking so fast. Can we not slow down a little?'

'What do you want to slow down for - do you wish to delay your destiny?' replied the old man with a critical tone in his voice.

'How can I delay my destiny when I don't know what it is? Besides, I don't have a Scroll of Destiny like you.'

'Mm...yes, so true. Okay then, a little slower for Lucy the Regular.'

Gabby then turned around and began to walk backwards. 'How's this?' he said with a grin.

Sophie shook her head.

'Why are the trees so many different colors of green?' Sophie was now walking almost face-to-face with the old man.

'Why shouldn't they be? Don't you like green or something? Or would you prefer to change the color?'

'No, I like green. It's how trees should be. It's just that back home I don't see as many greens.'

'Look, see here Lucy... it's all about looking.' Gabby began to sway his arms by his side as if he was doing a little dance as he walked backward. Not once did he turn his head to see where he was going. He seemed to be following the curve of the path perfectly as if he had eyes in the back of his head.

'I don't see what you mean?'

'Exactly - you don't see! Or rather, you only see according to how you look. The trees here are all shades of green because that's how *your* eyes and your brain interpret the color. Take me, for instance. I don't see just green trees but yellow, blue, purple, indigo, and rooby-dooby ones too! And I'm sure the animals here also see different colored trees.'

'Will I be able to see different coloured trees too?' asked Sophie excitedly.

'Maybe m'lady, if you learn to unlearn, and see like a bee,' replied the old man cryptically. He then leapt into the air and did a full 360 degree turn before carrying on walking backwards. Shortly after he clapped his hands and the light of the day vanished in an instant. Sophie was now walking under a night sky sprinkled with glittering speckles of stars. The stars also seemed to be shining brighter than Sophie had ever remembered seeing them before. Sometimes we are told to allow ourselves to be guided by a star, or stars. In the ancient past people navigated by the positions of the stars. So, when you see stars shining brighter than they've ever been, then you know some guiding force is not far away.

'Where has the day gone?!' exclaimed Sophie.

Gabby stopped walking and began to hop on one leg. 'The day has not gone anywhere, little Lucy. It is still here. And we are still here. Yet now it's time for the stars to be visible. And the stars are here all the time too, it's only that we don't see them when the sky is lit up. Both day and night are here always and ever - it just depends which one is in front. Now day is behind the night.'

The old man and Sophie both looked up into the sky. Overhead they could see shooting stars in almost all directions, fizzling and disappearing like sherbet rockets. Then Sophie began to hear some music. It sounded like strings being gently plucked. The sound was pleasant and soothing and seemed to vibrate amongst the stars in the sky.

'What's that music?'

Gabby turned to Sophie in surprise. 'You mean you don't know? Don't they teach you anything in the Regular World?!' All Sophie could do was shake her head and shrug. 'What you are hearing is the music of the spheres. It is the stars speaking to each other - theirs is the language of music. Down here language comes out as words, but up there amongst the stars the sounds are magnificent.' Gabby sighed as if lost in some reminiscence.

'Wow,' was all Sophie could say, as she stretched her head back to stare at the vastness above. When she turned around she could just faintly see Gabby in the starlight. He had a small book in his hands and he was reading through it. He looked up when he noticed Sophie watching him.

'I suppose you are hungry, little Lucy?'

As soon as he had said that Sophie realized that she had not eaten for so long and felt famished. 'It's Sophie. And yes, I am hungry now you mention it. I haven't eaten anything for ages.'

'Good. Then come with me and we shall meet our host for dinner.'

Before Sophie had time to answer, Gabby strolled off down the path. Sophie quickly followed for fear that she might lose sight of him in the dark. There was just enough light under the bright starry sky to see the old man and to also see the path beneath her feet. The path turned off to the right into a smaller one and soon they came to a small clearing where a respectable looking cottage stood. The lights were on and smoke could be seen spiraling up from the chimney. The cottage looked cosy and Sophie was eager for some comfort, despite feeling a little apprehensive. Where was she? And whose house was this? Without hesitation, Gabby strolled up to the door of the house and tapped gently. At the second tapping the door opened and a bulky figure stood in the doorway. Gabby, with his head bent down, suddenly looked frail and weak.

'Good sir, would you be kind enough to host a weary traveler and his young friend?' Gabby spoke in a meek voice as he pointed toward Sophie who stood a few meters behind.

The large man in the doorway smiled as he tugged on his bushy, dark beard.

'Why, of course, my dear traveler. Guests are always welcome here. Come, come, whoever you are. There is a warm fire here and food in the pot.' The large man stepped aside and ushered them both into his house. Inside was as cozy as cozy could be. The cottage was really just one big room that consisted of salon and kitchen, with a door leading off into what Sophie assumed was the main bedroom. She noted that it was a well-arranged and orderly house, full of pictures and ornaments all in their places. The stone walls reflected the shadows from the fire, licking warmth across the room like a friendly serpent.

The man introduced himself with a strange double name that Sophie could not understand at all. The confused look on her face made the man laugh.

'Just call me Gali,' he said. 'The friends that I still have call me Gali, and so can you.' Gali smiled and invited Sophie and Gabby to sit down at the table to eat. Sophie couldn't believe how ravenous she was. She tucked into the food as soon as it was placed in front of her and found it delicious. Gali smiled to see her enjoy his food.

'I'm glad you like my slunk stew!' said Gali as he poured another full ladle into Sophie's bowl.

Sophie peered at him from over her bowl. 'Slunk stew?'

'Yep. It's the slunkiest, stewiest stew you'll ever find this south-east of the Bogger Ridge Mountains,' replied Gali proudly. Sophie gulped. She wasn't sure if she even wanted to ask.

Gali turned out to be a jovial fellow, who listened intently to what the old man Gabby was saying whilst nodding his head and tugging on his bushy black beard. Sophie wished that she was more prepared for the journey and had felt silly that she was still wearing her pajamas. At least some normal clothes would have been more fitting. Lucky for her, she thought, that neither Gabby nor Gali had commented on her choice of clothes.

Gali, it turned out, was a man of many talents and skills. He was a philosopher, designer, and inventor, among other things. Right now, as he explained to Gabby and Sophie, he had invented the most spectacular telescope that allowed him to view life on other planets.

Gabby, it seemed, was most impressed and kept on asking to know more. The ragged old man, who spoke most eloquently when he wished to, paraded Gali with compliment after compliment. Gali's face was soon beaming with joy.

'Yes,' said Gali with his hands moving enthusiastically through the air, 'I can even see cities on Galimead, and objects moving about in the atmosphere. They have a whole civilization there I'm sure.' Gali spoke as excitedly as a young boy.

'Galimead?' Sophie shrugged. 'Where is that?'

Gali appeared to blush slightly, and lowered his head as he mumbled through his beard. 'Well, I named it that. I had to call it something. It seemed appropriate.'

'Right so, right so,' said Gabby nodding his head.

This made Gali cheer up once again. He began to explain how at this very moment he wanted to expand his research to investigate all the planets in the outer solar system, but that his instruments were not powerful enough. 'Alas,' he said with a shrug, 'I don't yet have the money or resources to make the research that will really change the worlds. Ahh…'

Sophie, feeling tired, excused herself and went to sleep in a corner of the room where Gali had arranged a bed for her. The two men, deep in conversation, talked and talked late into the night whilst Sophie slept. Or so it seemed that Sophie slept, for as soon as she had closed her eyes she found herself waking up again as daylight shone through the windows of the cottage. Her sleep, if that was what it was, had been no more than a blink of the eye. Perhaps, thought Sophie, a person does not sleep here in the Imaginal World. As Sophie sat at the breakfast table enjoying some home cooked bread and a hot mug of what Gali called 'Tattle Tea' - which tasted lovely and sweet - the two men continued talking like old friends. Gabby kept nodding his head excitedly as Gali talked about all his philosophical ideas and plans for new inventions. Sophie wouldn't be surprised if the both of them hadn't slept a wink.

'Well,' said Gabby as he wiped his mouth with his old bony fingers, 'this has been a real treat. Speaking with you Gali has fired my old bones. Yet we must be on our way. This young girl here has a quest and doesn't want to rest!'

Gali looked over at Sophie and nodded his head approvingly as if he understood perfectly the nature of quests. 'Well, my little friend, although we have spoken but few words between us it has been a pleasure having you in my house.' Gali spoke in a low voice that for Sophie resonated with kindness. 'I wish you well on your journey and may you find the source of your quest, whether it be at the beginning or the end.

Sophie nodded her head. 'Thank you, Gali. I wish you well too with your world watching and with your inventions. Maybe one day you can visit me in my house.'

'Perhaps, perhaps...in a century or two,' replied Gali whilst stroking his beard. 'Well, now I must pop out and cut some firewood. Please, be comfortable, and leave at your leisure.'

Gali stood up from the table, stretched his arms wide, and left the cottage humming. Sophie finished her breakfast in silence whilst Gabby appeared to busy himself with something.

'Are you ready? Come on, we need to go now, before he returns!' said Gabby hastily. It was only then that Sophie noticed that she was no longer wearing her pajamas but instead had on her jeans and a favorite yellow jumper.

'When did I...?'

'Go, go, go,' interrupted Gabby as he almost shoved her out the front door. Sophie turned around and was quick enough to see Gabby take a burning stick from the smoldering fire in the chimney and with it set alight the curtains of the cottage.

'Wheeeee!' screamed Gabby as he ran past Sophie, his thin legs moving rapidly as if racing a marathon. As he ran he leapt in the air with a fist punch, 'Yahweee...!'

Sophie was speechless and stood with her mouth open, not knowing what to do.

'Run, little Lucy, run!' yelled Gabby from further down the path.

Sophie looked back at the cottage and saw flames now coming out the windows. Soon the whole cottage would be alight and burnt to a cinder.

There wasn't much else to do - Sophie ran.

CHAPTER THREE – DARLING STARLING'S CURSE

If a reality isn't working for you, then what you need to do is change your ideas about reality

When Sophie finally caught up with Gabby he had stopped by the edge of a wide river and was doing a crazy little jig, punching the air erratically, and grinning inanely. Sophie was now sure the old man was a crazy lunatic - crazier than a goony loon.

'What...what...what have you done?!' stammered Sophie. She thought of poor Gali returning home with his firewood only to find his cottage burnt to the ground. 'Are you mad? Gali was so kind to us. He was, well, he was even your friend. You liked him, didn't you? Why did you burn his house down? You are so cruel - shame on you!' Sophie could hardly get the words out she was so mad. The old man stopped cavorting around and stood still with a solemn face. He then stuck his tongue out and blew a raspberry at Sophie.

'Poo you, Lucy! Didn't I tell you not to question what I do? Well?'

'Yes, but...'

'No buts. Not even a tiny half-but. I told you clear as is clear not to question my actions. If you can't agree to agree, then you have to leave right now.'

Sophie stood perplexed, not knowing what to do or say. She kept picturing in her mind the image of poor Gali and his cozy cottage all in a ruin.

'Stop those useless thoughts,' snapped Gabby. 'You're just wasting precious space in your head. Look!' The old man pointed across the river to a boat that was coming towards them from the far side.

'What is it?' Sophie squinted in the early light to see if she could see the boat more clearly.

'It's a butter-covered, pink rhino-bear, of course. Next useless question please!' Gabby tutted loudly.

Sophie was beginning to feel more than a little annoyed with this ragged crazy old man. She even had the fleeting idea to push him into the river for what he had done to poor Gali. When she next looked at Gabby he had such a sad look on his face that Sophie suddenly began to feel sorry for him, even though she had been angry just a moment earlier.

Gabby leapt onto the boat as soon as it had parked itself at the river's edge. Sophie instinctively followed and climbed onto what resembled a small ferry boat. They were the only two passengers on board. Sophie soon realized that there was no boat captain either - just the two of them on a boat that appeared to steer itself.

'How is it doing that?'

'Doing what?'

'Steering itself without a pilot, or driver, or whatever you call a person who steers a boat.' Sophie paced along the aisle between the empty benches of the boat.

'Oh, it's easy. You don't need a pilot, or driver, or a whatever-person,' giggled Gabby. 'We have boats that self-pilot themselves.'

'Really? How do they do it - by satellite?'

'Oh no, no,' said Gabby shaking his head. 'They don't need moons to steer them. They use electro-gravity.'

'Electro-gravity? You're just making this up!'

'Of course!' Gabby shrugged. 'How else do things work here in the Imaginal World...I thought you knew that?'

'Obviously not,' mumbled Sophie under her breath.

'Nice running shoes. I think I could do with a pair of those.'

Sophie looked down at her feet and saw that she was wearing her favorite pair of sporty running shoes. She couldn't remember when she had decided she wanted to be wearing them, although obviously it was a good decision based on her recent exploits. Then all of a sudden a wave of confusion and frustration swept over Sophie and she sat down, putting her elbows on her knees and her face in her hands.

'Gabby, I really don't know what I'm doing here. Everything now seems so confusing. I feel like I'm going nowhere.' Sophie let out a long sigh.

'But that's where you wanted to go, isn't it – to No-Where?' The old man sat with both legs dangling over the side of the boat.

'Yes, but…no, not that type of nowhere. I mean…ohh, I'm even confusing myself!'

'If it's to No-Where you wish to go, then to No-Where you shall go. Whether you ever arrive I cannot say - that's another matter.'

Sophie sighed. 'I don't think I'll ever reach No-Where, or No-Place. Maybe I'm not meant to, and this is all a game, or a puzzle or something.'

Gabby looked over at Sophie and began whistling a merry tune. 'Look Lucy. Lucy look and Lucy be lucky. If you want to reach No-Where you have to believe in it – to believe it's possible and be determined. No-Where is only unreachable for those who believe they can't reach it.'

Sophie looked over at the old man who seemed happy enough sitting on the side of the boat like a little kid. 'Are we going in the right direction now?' she asked.

'Mmm.' Gabby murmured and rolled his head. 'We're roundabout going in a straight line to where you need to be. Once we reach the Forest of Fernacles you take a southern-northerly direction and that will give you a circular path direct to No-Place. It's as simple as it is long, and no shorter!'

Sophie rolled her eyes. 'Thanks a bunch.'

When they had hopped off the boat at the other side of the river Sophie noticed that Gabby was wearing a new pair of white running shoes, just like her own. It looked odd to see a thin, ragged old man with a long straggly white beard and shabby clothes wearing the latest in sport shoes. Sophie quickly looked down to make sure she still had on her own running shoes, which she did.

'He's still a thief,' whispered Sophie to herself under her breath.

After walking some way from the river bank Gabby stopped and looked about in all directions.

'Where to now?' Sophie asked.

Gabby shrugged and pulled out the scroll of paper from inside his rags. After scanning the scroll briefly the old man turned to Sophie.

'There is someone we need to see first before we get to the Forest of Fernacles.'

'I hope it's not another house you need to burn down!' said Sophie sarcastically.

'Oh no, far from it, little Lucy,' replied Gabby with a goofy-tooth grin. He then sniffed the air like he was an animal smelling out prey. 'Er, I think it's going to be in this direction. Not that it matters, all roads lead to the same place.'

'Now I really know you're making all this up as you go along!'

The old man feigned a look of surprise. 'Aren't we all? You certainly are. I can tell you right now you have no idea what's going to happen next. And the writer of this book is making it up as he goes along as well.'

'What writer? What book? Are you talking about your paper of destiny, or whatever you call it?'

Gabby shook his head and sighed. 'Never mind. You'll find it all out for yourself...one day.'

The sunless bright sky shone over the day with a pleasant glow. Sophie again noticed that she felt neither hot nor cold. It felt like a goldilocks temperature - just right. She still could not understand where the warmth and light was coming from if there was no sun in the sky. Yet now she was learning neither to assume anything nor to expect any straight answers. And that is probably the best attitude to take. When in doubt, assume nothing – least of all any decent answers.

As the pair of them walked alongside the wide flowing river Sophie noticed that something was sticking out of the water and was moving, as if following them. As she continued to watch the strange object she was sure that it was moving parallel to them. And it looked like an elephant's trunk. Sometimes it would rise further out of the water, several feet high, before dropping down again. Gabby was strolling slightly ahead of Sophie, seemingly oblivious to his surroundings.

'What's that in the water?' Sophie could not contain her curiosity any longer.

'Mmm?'

'That thing there!' Sophie pointed her finger at the raised trunk in the water.

'Oh, that will be Nessie. Well, that's the name they gave her in the Regular World when she was there.' Gabby began to giggle uncontrollably, like a little boy.

'What's so funny?'

'They...hehehehe...they called her the Loch Ness Monster...haaaaaa! Imagine that, Nessie a monster! She's the sweetest, softest, most kind-hearted soul you'll ever meet. Anyway, she came back when people stopped believing in her. It's no fun to not be believed in. I mean, you believe you exist, don't you?' Gabby pointed a finger at Sophie.

'Well, sure I do. And you do too.'

'Do what?'

'Believe that you exist.'

'No, I don't.'

'What do you mean, you don't? You don't believe that you yourself exist?'

'That's right.' Gabby had now stopped walking and was facing Sophie with arms stubbornly folded across his chest.

'But how do you know if you exist or not? I don't get it?' Sophie looked perplexed.

'That's right. I *know* I exist. I don't need to believe it. If I chopped your leg off would you believe that it hurts or know that it hurts? Believing is one thing, and may serve you well for a time, yet knowing is another thing entirely. Just like most of your regular friends who didn't believe in Nessie - they didn't *know* the truth.' Gabby whistled a couple of times and the trunk in the water rose up, higher and higher. Sophie gasped as a huge creature emerged from the water, its long neck stretching several meters from the water's edge to where they were both standing.

'There, there, girl. Who's a sweetie, eh?' Gabby reached out his hand and tickled the huge head under its chin. A large smile appeared on the creature's face as its large eyes fluttered. The creature shook its head and water splattered into Sophie's face. She still could not believe her eyes.

'Nessie, say hello to little Lucy. She's never seen such a fine Apatosaurus like you before.' Nessie turned her head, which was small in comparison to the rest of her body, and ever so gently rubbed her face against Sophie. She was sure she heard a little purr come from Nessie's mouth. Sophie instantly felt safe with Nessie and reached out to touch her face. It was wet yet smooth, and the neck reached back several meters to her enormous body which was still standing in the river.

'Is she a dinosaur? I didn't think they still existed?' Sophie continued to stroke Nessie's head.

'The dinosaurs, as you call them, were in your Regular World a long, long time ago. That was in the early days. Sadly, they had to leave. Some of the brighter ones have stayed here in the Imaginal World for a while. Nessie here is one of them, and one of the cleverest dinos I know.' Nessie seemed to smile at that.

'Why did they have to leave? They told us at school that they all died out, became extinct.'

'I'm surprised you were listening in school,' Gabby said with a chuckle. 'Well, they couldn't dream. And if you can't dream, you can't keep any world going. Well, we had to learn. Don't worry though - we put them in a place which was far better for them.'

'So we need to keep dreaming...or we?' Sophie hesitated. She wasn't sure she wanted to know the alternative.

'Mm...' Gabby nodded his head thoughtfully. 'Dangerous as it is, it must be done.'

'Dangerous?'

'Oh, for sure. You see, your dreams will either trap you or free you – you have to choose which one it will be.' Gabby then suddenly smiled and clapped his hands. 'Well, we must be on our way otherwise we shall miss our encounter. Say goodbye to Nessie.'

Sophie stroked the creature's head one last time and watched as the huge shape sank back into the water.

'And you Regulars didn't think Apatosaurus's could swim. Ha, amateurs!' Gabby shook his head as he walked away.

They had been following the river's edge for most of the morning, turning off at the last minute to take a path that curved over a low hill. Sophie was beginning to wonder if there were any signs of civilization in this world - all she had ever seen were green fields and far-away mountains – when she spotted a woman preparing an outside table with food. Some nearby birds were hungrily howling like baby wolves when Gabby and Sophie approached the woman.

'A pleasant day to you madam,' said Gabby with a gentle bow. 'Surely is glorious to hear the singing birds at this time of year.'

'Indeed it is, kind sir. The howling birds remind me of the winters of my childhood. Such sweet sounds from their small beaks, just makes me fill with delight when I hear it,' replied a middle-aged lady with slightly fat arms. 'Would you travelers be hungry by any chance?'

The woman invited Gabby and Sophie to sit down at the picnic table which had been laid with a loaf of home-baked bread and assorted fruit. It seemed somewhat odd to Sophie why someone would wish to have a picnic at a table in the middle of an open field. The lady introduced herself as Ketav, a poor woman who made her living from mending and making shoes. Upon hearing this Gabby immediately took off his new running shoes and presented them to Ketav as a gift. Shortly after a young boy, looking only a year or two older than Sophie, came slouching up to the table and sat down without a word of greeting.

'This is my boy, my darling Starling, as I call him,' said Ketav. The young boy named Starling grunted as if he resented both his name and his mother's presence. He ate without a word and only occasionally cast a desultory glance across the table. Ketav, in her mild and simple manner, spoke of their hard life.

'Puh! You speak like a peasant woman,' snapped Starling. His young boyish features were hardened by a scowling face.

'We are peasants my dear. Yet we make the best of our life, and live

rich by the simple things. We don't need much to make us happy.'

'Maybe you don't. But I ain't like you. You think small things. I want to

be radical.'

Ketav smiled at her young son's words. 'Ah, that's my darling Starling -

always wanting to make things better. Maybe one day he will change

the world.'

After the simple lunch Gabby complimented Ketav once again on her

fine baking and got up to leave.

'Good sir, will you be kind enough to accompany my Starling to

yonder river and help him draw some fresh water. I fear he may do

something foolish if he goes by himself. Here, take this old and

battered bucket with you.'

'You are the foolish one, old bird.' Starling snorted in disgust and

walked off. Gabby bowed once more and, taking the bucket from

Ketav, agreed to do so.

'Don't worry, dear lady, your boy will be returned to you – as good as

new!'

Gabby and Sophie said their farewells to Ketav and went to catch up with the moody young boy.

As the three of them rounded the next hill they saw the fast flowing river weaving its way through the landscape. Gabby began whistling a jolly tune, which clearly annoyed the young boy, Starling. Nevertheless, he continued to whistle a tune that seemed to be getting louder and louder.

'Stop that damn noise, old man!' snapped the boy, obviously infuriated.

'Ah, but it's such a sweet day – don't you think so, darling Starling?'

The young boy stamped his foot. 'I'm not your darling! I'm not anyone's darling! It's just my damn, silly mother who says that. You watch, one day I'm gonna make you all pay.'

Gabby shook his head and tutted. 'My my, what an angry little demon you are.'

'Watch it old man, or you might regret it!'

Sophie didn't like the young boy one bit. It was as if he was filled with some nastiness; something eating away inside of him. Yet Sophie kept quiet and said nothing. They soon arrived by the river bank and found a suitable place to haul the water. Starling, his shoulders hunched and arms folded, looked about as eager as a corpse to do any water pulling. 'It looks like old Gabby is to fetch the water then?' Gabby looked over to the boy, who just shrugged and turned away. Gabby took the bucket and stood at the river's edge. 'Ah, what's that I see in the water – it looks like some gold coins! Let me get them.'

'Out the way, old man.' Suddenly the young boy brushed Gabby aside and peered into the water. He wasn't expecting what came next. Gabby gave the boy an almighty push from behind and he went flying into the river. Sophie heard a loud "splosh" as Starling hit the water and went under. He soon popped up again, his arms flailing and flapping as the strong currents of the river pushed him downstream. His screams and shouts came muffled above the noise of the river.

'I sure hope he doesn't poison the water with his foul tongue,' said Gabby nonchalantly as he strolled away. Sophie stood aghast, her jaw dropped open. She didn't know what to do, whether she should leap into the river to save the boy or shout at the old man. It was some moments before Sophie could collect herself enough to run after Gabby, who was now walking through the meadow with a new pair of sports shoes. By the time she had reached him she was out of breath and full of anguish. She didn't know whether she wanted to scream at him or try to drag him back to Ketav to confess his crime.

'You, you...you've maybe killed him. Starling could drown. You're crazy - you have to go back now and help him!'

Gabby just shook his head and kept on walking. 'Oh no, he's certainly a long way off by now. He won't drown, but he will be washed clean.' Gabby grinned as only an old man could.

'You're so cruel! You're in-human... you're...'

Gabby grabbed hold of Sophie's arm before she could say another word and gave her a hard stare.

'I told you at the beginning that you could only come with me if you didn't question my actions. You agreed to this!'

'Yes, yes...but that was before you did those...those terrible things. First Gali's house, now this...' Sophie felt exasperated, not knowing quite what to think or do.

'First you questioned me about my actions with Gali - and now here! You have proven yourself not yet ready to travel further with me.'

'I wouldn't want to travel any further with you anyway. You're a crazy old man!' cried out Sophie in a half-sob.

The old man became very serious. 'Now, let me tell you about the things you were unable to perceive, for there is more to events than surface appearances.' His grip on Sophie's arm loosened. 'When Gali searches through the ruins of his house he will find that a chest of treasure had been buried beneath the floor long ago. Without the fire Gali would never had discovered this treasure, and one day it would have been found by a less deserving person. With these new riches Gali will build for himself not only a new house but also a fine laboratory. He will be able to fund his research into observing the stars. As a consequence he will make many new discoveries that will benefit our thinking and imaginations. He will also invent and build an array of fine instruments for the betterment of science. Many of Gali's discoveries will eventually trickle down in idea and thought-forms into the Regular World where your folk will make great benefit from them. There will be more than one genius in your world who will owe all that they know to the work of Gali here. And all because of a house fire one day when Gali was out collecting wood. And Starling here…well, he's had a demonic curse on him since he was just a young baby. With such a curse raging within him he would one day kill his poor mother Ketav. Nor would he have stopped there either. And the worst of it is that his thoughts would have polluted the thought-forms in this world, damaging what we do here. These polluting thoughts would have entered the Regular World too, inspiring tyrants and dictators into war. In my Scroll of Destiny it was not for him to fulfill these wicked things. He needed to be cleansed of his accursed rage. The river will wash him far away, and will cleanse him too of his curse. It will take him much time to find his way back to his mother. Yet when he does, he will be a changed young boy. His personal journey will help him to grow up, and to be a considerate person. Like I said to his mother when we left, he shall be returned as good as new.'

Gabby let go of Sophie's arm and stepped back. Sophie was at a loss for words. The old man's wrinkled face softened and became gentle. 'It's okay, little one. You're not yet ready to see clearly. You all make the same fundamental mistake.'

'What's that?' asked Sophie quietly.

'People think their own way of seeing the world is the correct way – until they are proven wrong. Reality isn't as fixed as people think it is. If a reality isn't working for you, then what you need to do is change your ideas about reality.' As soon as he had said that he suddenly began to grow tall. A bright light engulfed his form that stretched upwards into a column of fire. Sophie fell backward onto the grass as a large flash made her lose her footing and almost blinded her.

Rubbing her eyes she saw before her a translucent, glowing figure in bright shimmering radiance. Sophie felt a mixture of fear and awe. She managed to make herself look up and when she did so she saw a smiling face of pure joy...and somewhere behind that radiant light was a shabby old man laughing. Then the blinding light disappeared and all went quiet. Sophie was alone again, sitting awkwardly on the grassy hill.

CHAPTER FOUR – THE FOREST OF FERNACLES

Remember, a closed door is not necessarily a locked door

Sophie was still in a half-daze as she strolled down the hill. All she could do was to follow her legs, even though she did not know where her legs were taking her. There are times when its best to let the body take over, as it usually knows best. Sophie walked on, still confused. From time to time she inadvertently looked up at the sky, as if expecting to see the old man Gabby flying overhead laughing. It took Sophie some time to recollect that she was on her way to find the Forest of Fernacles, whatever and wherever that was. For now, that was the only destination or guide she had for reaching No-Where, No-Place. As she looked about her it seemed that everything appeared so normal. And yet Sophie knew this was not the case. How could everything be so different from appearances? She didn't know whether it was the fault of her eyes in not being able to see things properly, or the fault of the Imaginal World for not letting her see how things actually were. In the Regular World things were pretty much as they appeared to be. Or, as people often used to say – 'it does what it says on the tin.' That was how people got along in the Regular World; you took things as you saw them. After all, wasn't it the case of believing things when you see them? Well, that type of thinking certainly had no place in the world where Sophie was now. And that, Sophie realized, could be a problem.

Sophie then remembered what Gabby had said about reality – that if it isn't working for you, then you need to change your ideas about reality. So Sophie told herself that from now on she would not think or compare realities, between this world and the world she had grown up in. It was then that she thought she saw a flicker of movement to the left, out of the corner of her eye. As she turned she saw something pass over the next hill. She immediately began to walk in the direction of the neighboring hill, hoping to meet someone who could perhaps guide her to the forest.

When Sophie reached the top of the hill she had a panorama view of all around her. However, as far as she could see there were hills in front of her, left and right, and a valley behind her – but not a forest to be seen. Then she heard an almighty squawk which made her jump and her heart skip a beat. Suddenly something ran past Sophie so fast and so close that it almost knocked her over. She swirled around to see what looked like a huge bird creature running on legs. It appeared to run around in circles squawking, flapping its bird-like wings but not flying. The creature made Sophie think of an emu, yet this creature had long thin reddish legs and bright yellow plumage and was standing upright just like a person. Sophie waved to the creature and shouted 'Hey!' After the third shout the creature looked up, hopped from leg to leg, then ran to where Sophie was standing and began to run circles around her too.

Soon Sophie began to feel dizzy. 'Hey, stop that!'

'What stop?' squeaked the creature in a high-pitched voice.

'Stop that running around me. You're making me feel ill.'

Suddenly the bird creature stopped still and placed its wings behind its back as it gave a bow. 'Why, of course, course of I will,' said the creature in a high-class gentleman's voice. 'All you had to do my dear was ask. Eddie at your service.'

'Well, er, thank you Eddie,' replied Sophie somewhat taken aback. She was not expecting this squawking bird to shift to a posh British accent.

'You look at me oddly, my dear. Is there something I should know - or has no one taught you how to blink?'

'I can blink!' said Sophie laughing. 'It's just that you look familiar, like some kind of a big bird.'

Eddie tutted. 'My dear child, I assure you, it is you who are the stranger one, believe me. Be assured we are the originals. Any other big birds are merely copies from our species. We realize there are other fakes out there in yonder worlds. Yet we,' said Eddie patting his chest, 'are the original Ganglies!'

'Ganglies?'

'Did I not pronounce some word correctly? Or is the windless air interfering with your ears, my child? Yes, we, including good sir Eddie here, are the original Ganglies. All others are poor imitations.' Eddie's face, with its large beak-for-a-nose, lit up in a huge grin.

Sophie reached out to touch Eddie the Gangly, wanting to see if he was real enough. Eddie instantly sprang to the side so Sophie's hand missed.

'Hey, hey, little girl from the other world - no touching Eddie til Eddie says to touch!'

'Oh sorry, I just wanted...'

'Wanted, wanted. You want so you reach out to take. Are you a politician or a politician's daughter?' Eddie slanted his large bird head to the side as if taking a right angle view of Sophie. Sophie realized that Eddie stood taller than herself, yet she didn't feel threatened by his presence.

'Actually, my father is an architect.'

'Arch - e – tect,' repeated Eddie slowly. 'I de-tect that your father likes arches - but does he like Ganglies?' Eddie flapped his large yellow-feathered wings.

'Dunno,' replied Sophie with a shrug. 'I doubt he's ever heard of a Gangly. But I'm sure he'd like you if he met you.'

'Not going to happen. Anyway, my fine unfeathered stranger, the question is - where are you going to?'

'I need to find No-Where, which is at No-Place. And I've been told that first I have to travel through the Forest of Fernacles.'

Eddie bowed his head. 'Mm...so you are one of those. You're not an accidental stranger at all. You're very much a deliberate stranger. And that makes all the difference.'

'Difference to what?'

'Difference to everything, of course! Difference to how we Ganglies treat you, to how the Forest of Fernacles will respond to you, and difference to everything on your journey. How could *you* be so indifferent to this?!' Eddie shook his head and squawked.

Sophie shook her head in confusion.

'Fear little or fear not, Eddie the Gangly will take you… er, what's your name, little unfeathered girl?'

SOPHIE'S SEARCH
FOR NO-WHERE

'Sophie.'

'Mm, well, better than Shuttlefart I suppose. So Eddie the Gangly will take you, Sophie, to the forest gate - the fernacles then are in your hands.'

Eddie turned around and gestured for Sophie to climb onto his back and told her to hold on tight around his neck. As soon as Sophie had climbed up Eddie started off with large hopping strides as he ran down, then up, then down, then up and down, one hill after another. 'I thought birds were supposed to fly,' shouted Sophie as they hopped along.

'I'm a Gangly bird - don't confuse your species!'

After what seemed like half a dozen hills and countless long-legged hops Eddie finally stopped on top of a particularly large and steep hill. Sophie climbed down and looked around. She could see nothing except even more hills.

'I don't see any forest. Where are we?'

Eddie tutted and shook his big head and grinned from almost ear to ear. He then lifted up his wings and as he did so two human-looking hands seemed to appear out of them. Eddie made three loud claps with these hands before they retreated again into his winged plumage. The large Gangly laughed as he saw the amazed look on Sophie's face.

'Turn around, do not look at the floor but behold the door.'

Sophie turned around and saw a large green door in front of her, hovering about a foot off the ground. Sophie hesitated, not sure what to do. She turned back to look at Eddie who was now gently rocking from one large bird foot to the other.

'Well, So-fe, are you going to walk through the door or not? No one else can do it for you. Remember, a closed door is not necessarily a locked door.' And saying that, Eddie swiftly turned around and began bounding away in huge leaps.

Sophie reached up to the knob on the green door and turned it. The door first moved with a slight creak and then glided open effortlessly. Sophie peered in through the open door, yet all she could see on the other side was just a haze, a swirling type of fog. Not knowing what else to do, Sophie put her right foot forward, as if upon a step. On the other side of the green door she felt what appeared to be steps in front of her. So she hesitantly began to climb them. Suddenly the steps began to move, as if they were some sort of escalator. Sophie wobbled to one side and instinctively reached out to grab hold of something.

She caught what she felt to be a handrail at the side of the invisible

steps. The steps then began to move very fast, and the swirling fog was

now blowing through her hair. Sophie began to feel a little dizzy,

disorientated, as she couldn't see where she was going. So Sophie

closed her eyes tight and held firmly onto the handrail with both

hands. As soon as she was sure the steps could move no faster they

began to slow down and finally came to a gentle stop. When Sophie

opened her eyes again she found herself to be standing in a small

clearing in the middle of a forest. She immediately knew there was

something odd about the forest - something very different. And then it

hit her - the forest was blue!

'This can't be right...a blue forest!' There are some things which just

don't *feel* right, such as a Saturday being in the middle of the week; or

putting green ketchup on your potatoes. And a blue forest was one of

those not-quite-right-things…Then Sophie realized that she shouldn't

be comparing what she saw here with what she knew back in her own

Regular World. Things were indeed different in the Imaginal World. If

there was one thing Sophie could be sure about, it was to expect the unexpected. And what do you naturally do when faced with the unexpected? Well, you move on of course.

Ahead of her, at the edge of the clearing, Sophie saw a path that led into the forest of blue trees. Despite the strangeness of the forest she did not feel threatened, just slightly apprehensive. As she entered the forest path and began walking she saw that light was streaming through from above the trees and covered the forest with a bluish glow. Then Sophie realized another thing which had been puzzling her from the start but which hadn't troubled her until now – the smell. It was a familiar smell; one that made her think of being back home in the kitchen with her mother cooking. Fish…raw fish! That was it – the Forest of Fernacles, with its blue trees, smelt of fresh fish. And yet there was not a fishy thing in sight, or sound. Sophie, now feeling increasingly curious, continued along the path. On both sides she saw bushes of strangely mixed hues of blue, the like she had never seen before in nature. It all looked strangely appealing, despite it being so out of place.

Sophie walked further into the forest, gazing in amazement at the oddity of it all. Everything around her looked like a normal forest back home – the trees, shrubs, etc – and yet her senses confused her. Her eyes could only see a *blue* forest, and her nose could only smell the *fishyness*. It was a weird mix of the familiar with the strange, and it made her feel out of place. Not that this was any new feeling since entering the Imaginal World. Yet the thing that kept driving her onwards, further into the forest and even further beyond, was the goal – the *need* – to seek for No-Where in No-Place. With this in the forefront of her mind Sophie pushed on, following the winding path ahead. As she strolled, her eyes scanned the blue environment around her. Suddenly, at the side of the path, she noticed a big rock with the words 'Lift Me' written upon it.

'How can I lift such a big rock myself?' thought Sophie. And yet, a part of her also knew that anything was possible in this world. Yet just because a thing is possible it doesn't mean we should go and do it. That's the problem with written orders – such as 'Lift Me' – we tend to automatically respond to them. And the fact that it was written on a large rock made the proposition so much more enticing. How could anyone resist such an offer?…which, of course, is part of the problem in the Regular World. So, just because it was likely to be possible – and because the large rock said so – Sophie bent down to lift it up. Sure enough, the rock lifted up in her hands like papier-mâché. Beneath the rock was a large dark and dingy hole and nothing else, or so it seemed.

SOPHIE'S SEARCH
FOR NO-WHERE

Sophie peered in, trying to make out anything in the darkness. She suddenly jumped back as a long, scaly, slithery thing slinked out of the hole. If Sophie had to guess quickly then what she now saw rise up before her was an overweight worm with a greasy, blubbering fat man's head, with pimples ready to be squished. She stepped back, gulping, as her stomach churned in squeamish revulsion. The slithery thing stretched up to the height of an adult, and then peered down with glassy eyes upon the now frozen Sophie.

'Shank you, little girl,' slobbered the slithery, globular head.

'Er,' stammered Sophie, aghast. She wasn't sure if she should run now or talk to the thing.

'Is shat your name, little girl - Er?'

'Er, no. I mean, my name is Sophie,' said Sophie a little hesitantly.

'Ah, shuch a sweetly name is that for a little girl. And you ish not from around here, ish you?'

'No, I'm not. I'm, er, from what you would call the Regular World.' The worm's greedy little eyes lit up. 'Ah, she's from the Regular World. How delightful ish that...mm.'

Sophie didn't like the look, or the sound, of this thing, and felt she needed to get away as quickly as she could. She looked around her.

There were nothing but blue trees and blue-hued shrubs. So she knew she had to keep her cool.

'And what's your name? And who are you?' Sophie looked directly into the worm's eyes, watching him carefully.

The slimy worm wriggled its fat, pimple-pecked face. 'A Harkone issh what I am. And my name, if it please you, issh Borik.' The worm then raised itself high upon its slithery haunches and slurped its lips. 'Shanks sho much for releasing me from under the rock.'

'Well, it did say "Lift Me",' replied Sophie with a shrug.

Borik the Harkone waggled its fat head. 'Sho it did. Sho it did.'

'It's been, er, interesting to meet you, Borik, but I must go now.'

Borik slithered in front of Sophie and blocked her path. 'And where does the little girl Sophie shink she's going?'

'I'm on my way to No-where.' Sophie stood her ground, and yet her heart was now pounding hard in her chest.

'No-where?'

'Er, yes, it's at No-Place.'

Borik's head continued to waggle from side to side. 'Well, if you're going nowhere then whatsh the rush, little Sophie? Here ish as good as nowhere.' The worm creature tried to grin but only ended up slobbering.

SOPHIE'S SEARCH
FOR NO-WHERE

'I'm looking for a different nowhere…and I think it's that way,' said

Sophie pointing ahead as she made to step forward. Borik again quickly

blocked her path and slurped his lips together in a way that Sophie

thought was disgusting.

'Not sho fast, sweet, delicious little girl.' Borik grinned and a globule of

yellow saliva-pus dripped from his rubbery lips.

'And why not so fast - is there a speed limit in this forest?'

Borik swayed his head from side to side and feigned an apologetic sigh.

'No…but itsh like this you see - I have to eat you. Shorry, little regular

girl.'

All of a sudden the blue Forest of Fernacles didn't seem so pleasant

after all; nor did the blueness seem so welcomingly blue. And the fish

smell was now fishier than ever.

'What! Eat me? Why, what have I done?'

Borik swayed his greasy, fat head, and his puffed-up nose snorted. For

a brief moment Sophie was sure Borik had the face of a politician she

had once seen on television making a speech. 'You've done nothing…

if you wissh to know.'

'But…but I lifted the rock and saved you. I helped you!' Sophie's voice was now beginning to wobble. It was like a bad dream. No worse…worse than a bad dream.

'Mm, yesh, maybe you did. But you see, itsh like this – I eat people. It's what I do. It's my nature, like it or lump it.' Saying that, Borik gave out a horrendously loud burp and his whole, long slimy body rippled like a scaly wave.

An anger of injustice rose within Sophie that momentarily overtook her fear. 'But that's not fair – I lifted the rock that said "Lift Me" written on it!'

Borik's fat, greasy face burst into a repugnant laugh, and he burped a second time. 'Yesh, yesh, but you didn't *have to* lift it did you, you shilly fool. Do you always do what words tell you, eh? If it said "Jump into a mud volcano" – would you do it, eh?'

'Of course not! That's stupid,' replied Sophie in a now petulant tone.

'Its not sshtupid. You're the sshtupid one for doing whatever you read, little girl. And now I'm gonna eat you because that's what I do. It just *is*. Got it? Stop complaining like a ferkle frump!'

Borik lurched forward toward Sophie with a huge fat face-splitting grin. Sophie instinctively jumped to one side and then ran past Borik, hoping to get down the path fast enough so Borik couldn't follow. Yet as soon as she had sped past Borik's body she felt herself being grabbed by the legs and lifted swiftly off the floor. She was caught in Borik's tail and was wrapped around several times, hanging several feet from the ground. Borik now shuffled down the path, humming and slurping to himself.

'Where are you taking me, let go of me you fat, greasy worm!' screamed Sophie, now frantic. Her heart was pumping so fast so thought it might explode through her chest.

'Shticks and sstones may blubber my bones but names will never, blah blah blah. Mm, shuperlicious dish, ish you,' replied Borik as he curled and slithered his way down the path, further into the dense blue Forest of Fernacles. The further they went into the forest, the more it smelt of raw fish.

'But you can't eat me. I'm a human...a real human.'

'Yeshh, I know, you will have a bad after taste. Oh well!' Borik let out an exaggerated deep sigh.

'No, you can't! This isn't real. This world isn't real,' Sophie cried out. She still couldn't believe any of this was happening. Wasn't it only a dream after all?

'No. No, it ish real. I eat you here, and you don't return to the Regular

World. Another little girl who went missing. It happens all the time.

Your world is full of missing little children. Some of you come

here...dreaming your littleish childish dreams. And bumf - you never go

back. We got ya!...shslum shslum, shslum shslum shslum.' If Harkones

could whistle they would. But they cannot - and so they slurp and slosh

instead. The globules of spit and saliva dripped down the pimpled

pock-marked face of Borik. His weasel eyes were set back in folds of

fat. His face looked like that of a man who had never grown up, nor

ever shaved. A boyish immaturity in the face of a fat, greedy man -

stuck on the end of the huge slithery body of a worm.

'You're worse than a fat cat,' mumbled Sophie under her breath.

Sophie was now finding it hard to fight back the tears. 'But I have to

find No-Where!'

Borik appeared nonplussed by all the fuss. 'But that's exactly where

you're going, little girl – nowhere!' Borik's laughter came out in slurps

and slops.

'No – my No-Where! It's my mission. I have to get there!' Sophie was

trying to wriggle, to free her arms, yet to no avail. Borik's tail was

wrapped tightly around her and there was no escape.

'Mission smission! You're just another dreamer, like all the rest. You have your shilly dreams that you shink are important. But it's all a shilly fantasy - and you get eaten in the end. You shink here it's all fairy castles and princeshess...shilly billies.' And with a nimble flick and swoosh of his tail Borik fastened Sophie's legs to a hanging blue vine from a Fernacle tree. He then began to slither away, leaving Sophie hanging upside down.

'Hey! Hey, what's going on?' If it was one thing Sophie didn't like, it was being left to hang upside down.

'Going to look for other shings to cook you with - not want nashty tashte in mouth.' Borik slurped and slithered down the path and out of sight. As soon as he had disappeared through the trees a great stillness seemed to enter the forest. Sophie, hanging upside down with her feet fastened tight to a vine, felt the blood rush to her head. Seconds faded into minutes all too slowly for Sophie. From her upside-down perspective Sophie became aware that the lightness of the forest was dimming.

Soon the whole forest had sunk into darkness. And that was when the colors changed. As soon as darkness came to the Forest of Fernacles, so too did the shimmering, translucent blueness. All the blue trees of the forest lit up as if glowing from the inside. The whole forest sparkled with various hues of blues, like an ocean rippling through. It could have been a beautiful sight, if Sophie was not hanging upside down and straining to see all the colors with a bent neck. She then sniffed the air.

'At least the fish smell is gone. Nothing worse I guess than being eaten with the smell of wet fish.' Sophie was muttering out loud to herself. It seems a natural human tendency to talk to oneself when in trouble, as if talking-to-self mode will allow one to find an escape plan or, at the very least, hide the fact of one's impending dilemma.

Sophie was right, however; the fishy smell had now been replaced by an odd perfumery smell that wafted through the blue fluorescent forest.

'Mm...damned if I'm hanging around for this. I'm not getting eaten by that fat blob Borik.' With renewed determination Sophie tried reaching up to where her legs were tied. She could reach the vine, yet it was too tightly twisted around her legs to loosen, and was pulled even tighter by the gravity of her weight.

'Come on, Sophie! Come on!' she half-screamed to herself, wriggling even more. And yet the wriggling just served to tighten further the vine around her legs. 'Ah, what a snot-blob of a mess I'm in!'

Hanging upside down, a foot or so off the floor, did not give Sophie much of a perspective on things. And her neck was now beginning to hurt from all the straining. She sighed and closed her eyes. She tried to find that inner silent space where she always retreated to when she needed to find strength. It was a special place deep inside of her that nobody knew about. From this special place she could listen to a voice that spoke to her; a familiar voice that Sophie felt she had always known. In this private inner space she found comfort and strength. So she listened within, and listened hard, trusting in the voice that always came. Sophie remembered her own advice she once gave herself: *When in doubt, listen within. And when in real doubt, don't do anything that later you'll regret as being stupid.* So she remained quiet, not doing anything that she might later regret as being somewhat stupid (such as lifting a rock that says "Lift Me"!). Sophie listened hard…and then strained to listen even harder. She was almost out of listening strength when…

…when she thought she heard something. It was faint at first, and then grew louder. Yet it wasn't her familiar inner voice - it was something completely different.

Huff, huff, huff, huff, huff, huff, huff, huff, huff, huff, huff, huff…

Huff, huff, huff, huff, huff…came a sound from within the forest not too far away. Sophie remained hanging, eyes closed, concentrating on staying calm and listening. And there it was again…

Huff, huff, huff, huff, huff, huff, huff, huff, huff, huff, huff, huff…

The huffing was gentle, soft, and almost hypnotic, as if the sound was being carried along on cushions. And now the sound was getting louder, coming closer. Sophie knew it could not be Borik, that slurping-slither of a blob-worm. Finally, it sounded as if the huffing was right in front of her, or beneath her, or thereabouts.

The huff huffing climaxed into a long drawn out huufffff - and then silence.

'Huff?'

Sophie opened her eyes, which were a foot away from the forest floor. And she came face to face – or rather eye-to-eye - with a bright blue-eyed fluffy face.

'Huff?'

'Hello,' Sophie said smiling.

'Huufff, huff, huff?!'

Sophie nodded her head, which was slightly difficult considering she was hanging upside down. 'Yes, I am in a kind of trouble. Do you think you could help me?'

The fluffy face leaned forward until its nose was touching her forehead, and then it sniffed. Its nose twitched, and then sniffed again. 'Huff, huff, huuffff?'

'Yes, it is somewhat uncomfortable hanging upside down. Believe me, it's not something I would recommend.'

A whole series of huffing and a shuffling of feet erupted around her. From her upside down position Sophie could now see a whole row of furry creatures in front of her. Upside down furry heads attached to furry arms that were all crossed, sitting on furry feet with claws. Now Sophie was really beginning to feel dizzy. It felt as if the blood that had previously rushed to her head was now involved in a swimming race. 'Ohhh…I don't feel so good. Do you think you could, er, kind of untie me?'

'Hufff, huff!'

Sophie felt a whole patter of tiny feet climbing up over her body, light and dexterous. A band of fluffy little creatures then proceeded to untie her legs from the vine whilst huffing gently together in rhythm. Sophie

fell to the floor in a heap, then let out a huge sigh of relief.

'Oh, thank my stars for that.'

'Not stars - huffalots.' The first little fluffy creature smiled and waggled

its head from side to side in a way that made Sophie laugh.

'What...huffalots?'

The little creature again waggled its head from side to side, which

seemed to be an affirmative gesture. 'Yes, huffalots. I huffalot, he

huffalot, they huffalots, we huffalots.'

Sophie squinted and looked closely at the small blue-eyed, grey-furry

creature. Then it struck her – the blue-eyed creature had just one huge

blue eye in the centre of its forehead. Suddenly it blinked at her. The

fluffy creature looked similar to a cross between a squirrel and a rabbit,

and was hunched on two back legs, with two front paws in a crossed-

arm position. All the little creatures - all the huffalots - looked identical.

All their blue eyes were shining and blinking, giving the impression of

fairy lights flashing on and off. As she looked around at the huffalots,

each one smiled in return and gave a soft 'huff.'

'You all look the same! Oh, forgive me, I didn't mean to be rude by

that.'

'Not rude,' said the huffalot who had spoken first. 'Huffalots all same. One huffalot, all huffalots - I huffalot, he huffalot, they huffalots, we huffalots. One huff for each, one huff for all.

'Well, thank you huffalots for getting me down. I was starting to feel queasy.

All the huffalots now waggled their heads from side to side in one synchronized motion and all huffed gently together.

'We huffalots happy to help nice smelling girl. What we do next?'

Sophie looked around her anxiously, now realizing that Borik could return at any moment. The blue translucent forest was deceptive in its beauty, for it also held unknown threats and uncertainties. She shook her head, as if attempting to shake her memory back into focus.

'Ah, what am I doing!' Sophie called out half to herself and half to the forest.

'You dreaming, little girl. You need to dream harder. You losing the dream. You going nowhere.'

All the huffalots wiggled their heads side to side unanimously.

'Yes - that's it! I have to find No-Where, at No-Place. Can you help me - quickly, before Borik the Harkone returns?'

As soon as she had said the Harkone's name, all the little huffalots swayed back on their hunches together and rolled their one big blue eye in unison. Then they all let out a great, almighty HUFF!

The first huffalot turned to his fellow huffalots and gave out a few short, yet no doubt meaningful, *huffs*. All the little huffalots huffed together and wiggle-waggled their heads.

'Borik the Harkone no good. Tricky little trickster – he smell bad. He dream bad too. Forest not like him. We go quick. Best way to No-Where from here is by water, not land. We huffalots take you to lake-that-is-an-ocean. Okay, little girl?'

Sophie nodded. 'Yes, please! And my name is Sophie.'

'We go, So-Fe. Huff, huff, *hufffffff*.'

Several of the little huffalots picked up Sophie and lay her back onto a bed of huffalots that then began to run through the forest, away from the path. Sophie was being bobbed around, yet she felt secure in the huffalots grip. She swayed and moved up and down as the bed of huffalots beneath her scampered through the forest floor, dodging shrubs and blue fernacle tree branches.

Suddenly a loud hissing and spitting noise pierced through the air as behind them a very annoyed Borik began pursuit.

'Heysh, come back! You sshtealing my food!'

'Huff, huff, huff, huffffff.'

The huffalots all huffed together and picked up the pace as the sound of breaking shrubs came from behind them. Borik was fast slithering his way through the tangle of forest, determined to catch up with the scampering huffalots. Sophie was unable to do anything, relying totally upon the speed and ingenuity of the huffalots beneath her. And there was a lot of huffing coming from below. It was now a race between the small band of huffalots and the slithering worm Borik the Harkone. The shimmering shades of blue glowed past her, making Sophie feel as if she was in some fantastical video game. Below her she also saw the many different blue-colored shrubs as they brushed past the darting bodies of the fluffy huffalots.

After a time the dense blue forest seemed to thin out until finally, leaving it behind, they came upon a sparkling lake of many shades of blue. In front of them stood a wooden jetty that had a sail boat moored at the end of it. The huffalots ran huff huffing along the jetty and, arriving at the sail boat, gave out a unanimous huge *huffff*. They placed Sophie on her feet and, pushing her from behind, almost threw her onto the boat.

'Dream harder, dream faster, dream bigger!' said one of the huffalots at the front. Sophie couldn't be sure if it was the same creature who had spoken to her before. Indeed, they all did seem alike.

'I will,' replied Sophie, exhausted and out of breath. And then she fell back as the boat pulled away. 'Thank you, huffalots!'

All the huffalots blinked their huge blue eye and bowed together with a collective *HUFF*. They then turned and scampered away into the forest just as Borik emerged.

'Yahhhh! Snot fair, snot fair! You're my food. I'm hungry - come back. I promise not to eat all of you!'

Borik the Harkone drooled and slobbered, and raged. The huffalots were nowhere to be seen. And Sophie slumped onto one of the ship's wooden benches, feeling completely worn out, and closed her eyes.

CHAPTER FIVE – THE-LAKE-THAT-IS-AN-OCEAN

No-Where is only unreachable for those who believe they can't reach it

When Sophie opened her eyes again she found herself to be on a boat that was rocking gently in a breeze under a blue-green sky. She looked up through the sails and saw fluffy white clouds drifting overhead like lost pieces of some cut-out jigsaw. Sophie stood up and leaned to look over the side of the boat. She gasped. All that could be seen, in all directions, was water…no land anywhere.

'But how could that be – it was just a lake a moment ago!' she said out loud.

'Aye, it's the lake-that-is-an-ocean. That's what it is, missy. Aye, lake-that-is-an-ocean.'

Sophie swung around to see where the voice had come from. In her exhaustion, and then her waking daze, she had not even looked to see who was captaining the boat. The deck of the sail boat was around fifteen meters long and was polished wood. It was the kind of boat they don't make any more, and looked spanking brand new. As she looked around further Sophie now noticed that the whole boat, and not just the deck, was made from polished wood, the color of setting sun.

'Aye, missy, over 'ere I be…come see Captain Jimbob, aye.'

Sophie walked past the large wooden mast that stood tall in the centre of the boat, and then she noticed a platform that rose above a few steps. All she could see was a figure in a blue uniform with a white cap that was hidden behind a large wheel. Sophie climbed the steps and walked toward the figure.

'Aye, welcome to my boat, missy. I be Jimbob, and this ere is ma boat. Called *Pussin Water* she is, and a fine girl she be, missy.'

'My name's Sophie.'

'Aye missy, Sophie you be, and welcome aboard ma *Pussin Water*.

'Thank you.' Sophie stepped forward to get a better view of Captain Jimbob, as she could only see some brown hair curling out from under the white cap. Sophie's eyes widened. 'But you're a dog!'

Jimbob chuckled and pulled out the pipe from his mouth. 'No missy Sophie, I be a Sproggit. And I be the oldest Sproggit there be, mind yer that.' And with that he popped the unlit pipe back into his mouth and puffed. Nothing came out.

'Well, you look just like a Yorkshire terrier dog to me.'

Jimbob looked askew at Sophie. 'A *your-shoe-tear-here*? Could a *your-shoe-tear-here* do this?' The captain began to sway his knees in and out as if doing some strange dance.

Sophie laughed. 'No, dogs don't dance, or walk upright on two feet.'

'Aye, there you is then, like I say, missy Sophie. I be Jimbob the oldest Sproggit. And you be mistaking things from yer yonder Regular World. Here, you live your dreams - you don't sleep them into existence.'

Sophie suddenly remembered where she was supposed to be heading. 'It's No-Where that I have to find. I have to reach No-Where by getting to No-Place. I remember now, the huffalots said I could get there from the lake-that-is-an-ocean. How long will it take us to get there?'

Jimbob scratched his furry cheek and winced. 'Well now, you're on the road to No-Where, eh? Aye, that be a tricky one, missy Sophie. That all be depending on which way yonder wind blows. We could either get to No-Where from 'ere or find No-Place from over there.'

Sophie sunk her head in her hands. 'Oh, we'll never reach it. It's just a game – all a game. I'm getting nowhere!'

Jimbob puffed on his empty pipe. 'Aye, that be the plan, missy. Look 'ere missy Sophie, No-Where is only unreachable for those who believe they can't reach it. You've gotta have the intention, missy. Remember, we don't do straight things here in the Imaginal World. We be rounded, circular, and yet here all ends meet. Here, everything has its purpose, and everything is connected. Aye, it is. It's the same in your world too – you just don't see it that way. You look at everything separate and straight...aye, it's a funny thing, but you do it.' Jimbob went back to steering the boat.

Sophie didn't know what else to say, so she walked to the back of the boat and sat down. How could she ever get to No-Where or No-Place if she didn't know what it was, where it was, or even the slightest clue of how to get there? She was just following a...a dream! Then Sophie laughed to herself. It was indeed all a dream; all some kind of play, and now she was a part of it – here in the Imaginal World. And what had the Green Man said? In dreams begin responsibilities...

Sophie stood up and marched over to where Jimbob was steering the boat.

SOPHIE'S SEARCH
FOR NO-WHERE

'Jimbob, tell me – what's the next step we need to take in order to get closer to No-Place?'

Jimbob grinned, and a small set of pointy teeth shone from inside his mouth. 'Aye, that be right, missy Sophie. We would need to be heading in that direction.' And Jimbob pointed with his pipe to his left.

'Then take us in that direction, and focus on it, Jimbob. We don't have time to dream on it!' Sophie had spoken as if she was now captain of the boat.

'Aye aye, missy. Here we go.' Jimbob pulled on the large wooden wheel of the boat and swung her around. The sails above flapped in resistance to the wind as they shifted the boat's position. 'So why you be going to find No-Where, missy Sophie? You've gone and lost your dreams?'

Sophie hesitated for a moment. 'I can't say exactly. It's not something I can put into words. I was always traveling somewhere in my dreams, ever since I was a little girl. I always knew my dreams were important. Then...well, then *something* invited me in, and I knew I had a purpose. It's like I feel that the dreams need me. Does that sound odd to you?'

Jimbob puffed on his pipe and blew out air. 'Nope, sure don't. It all sounds about right to me. Dreams are as real as anything else. People in the Regular World think they are not dreaming when they call themselves "awake"…but there is no awake, it's all part of the dream. It's just that sometimes we dream deeper, and we dream our part, and we play our part. Just to ignore the dreaming is no good. Why, missy, it brings no meaning! The Regular World doesn't know what real meaning is, so it has to invent it, with silly ideas. Aye, they just have no real imagination…and no ultimate meaning, mystery, or magic. Missy Sophie, do you know what an unfathomable mystery is? And what would you do if you encountered one?'

Sophie paused and looked out over the expanse of water. She suddenly imagined herself being so tiny, on a tiny unreal boat inside a huge plastic dome bubble, like the ones people shake to make snow fall or water glitter. And maybe someone soon is going to take a big hand, lift up their plastic bubble, and shake it so hard everything splashes everywhere and water runs up. And then maybe, just maybe, Sophie would wake up having forgotten all about her journey and the quest for No-Where in No-Place.

'I think life is one great mystery – and how we encounter it gives us our meaning,' Sophie said softly.

SOPHIE'S SEARCH
FOR NO-WHERE

Jimbob grinned and pointed to a wooden chest on the front deck.

Sophie opened it and saw it was full of white captain's caps, just as

Jimbob was wearing. She took one and placed it on her head, captain-

like. Now she was taking charge, and making a direction for herself.

She looked out over the expanse of water that was the lake-that-is-an-

ocean, and noted all the subtleties of color that were reflecting off it.

She, or rather the boat, appeared to be in the middle of nowhere. How

ironic! And yet for perhaps the first time in a long time, Sophie felt

within her a real purpose. It felt like a tight ball, strong yet light,

bouncing around in her chest like a gyroscope – or compass.

'I am my own compass now, and I'm in charge. Nothing's going to get

in my way now,' she whispered to the breeze.

No sooner had she said that did Sophie sense a sudden change in the

air, as if some mind in the clouds had heard her own whisper. The light

breeze began to rise…first into the sails, then across the whole boat,

and finally it blew through Sophie's hair. And it rose, and rose; and for

the first time waves sprung up and glided across the surface of the

water. The pleasant blue-greenish sky lost its radiance, and dark

shadows crawled in overhead. Sophie knew this was not good news.

She made a dash for the front of the boat. Jimbob was sucking on his smokeless pipe and squinting at the horizon.

'Aye, missy, we got one of those yonder storms breaking in. Better we get fixed up good and ready to ride her out. Here, grab the wheel, and keep *Pussin Water* heading yonder.'

Before Sophie could respond Jimbob had thrust the large wooden ship's wheel into her hands and sprung off on his two strong hairy legs. Sophie could barely manage to keep the wheel straight as it fiercely tugged against her grip. She could hear Jimbob shouting to her as the wind now whipped around her head.

'Keep 'er steady Sophie, keep 'er steady now.'

Sophie could barely keep her attention on Jimbob who was winching the sails and bringing them down before the storm ripped them apart.

'I'm trying…it's pulling me!' shouted Sophie.

Just then the wheel was ripped out of her hands as the boat lurched suddenly to the side with a tremendous force. Sophie fell to the floor and rolled to the side of the deck. She quickly got to her feet, and was suddenly thrown again to the floor as the boat lurched to the other side. A fierce rain began to lash down, soaking Sophie to the skin. Yet this only added to the water that was now splashing over the side of the boat as it began to roll and heave from side to side. Sophie was being tossed from one side to the other, as the wheel – and the boat – was now clearly out of control.

A wet, dog-eared figure scrambled up the steps onto the upper platform. Jimbob the Oldest Sproggit looked as if he had just tumbled out of a washing machine. Amazingly, his white captain's cap was still perched on his head. He scurried over to where Sophie was huddled beside one of the benches.

'What yer be doing with your mind, Sophie?'

'What do you mean?' replied a very confused Sophie.

'Yer thoughts missy, they're brewing up a storm!'

'But I didn't do anything!'

Jimbob grabbed the side of the boat and peered over. His clenched mouth suddenly dropped open and his pipe fell to the floor. He staggered back to where Sophie was hanging on. 'It's a whirly-worm hole – and it's a big 'en! Better grab on tight missy, this ain't gonna be pretty…aye. Come on *Pussin Water*, yer can make it now, lassy.'

Jimbob fought through the sideways lashing rain to reach the large wooden steering wheel that was now spinning furiously. He grabbed onto it and with all his strength and weight attempted to bring its roulette craziness under control. His captain's uniform and white cap was stuck wet to his skinny frame. Sophie thought he looked so ragged and fragile, his face worn and determined. Jimbob's dogged dog-brown eyes stared ruthlessly into the rain as his face strained under the pressure of struggling with the almighty elements of the storm. Sophie watched on as she sat huddled down by one of the benches, cowering from the storm. Jimbob looked over to her, and a little snarl curled his lips.

'Get ye over 'ere, missy. The only way to survive is by facing yer fear. Fear not, and live true – come on, missy Sophie. Step up to it!'

Sophie gritted her teeth and pulled herself up so that she was now receiving the full force of the storm. Amidst the furious noise of the wind and the rain she called to the place of inner quiet within her. She concentrated to remain calm as she staggered across the deck of the swaying boat. On reaching Jimbob at the wheel she grabbed on and exerted her full force to keep it from jerking about wildly. She looked at Jimbob through wet streaming eyes and saw him grinning at her. Like two drenched actors in the spinning fury of a play, they raged against the elements.

'Hold 'er steady and straight…we're heading for the centre of the whirly-worm hole. We must ride 'er true. We can't lose *Pussin Water!*'

Sophie let go of all thoughts – all fears – and focused hard on the task at hand: to keep the boat steady and straight as they headed into the true centre of the giant watery worm hole. The boat suddenly lurched forward and then tipped down front end, with the rear of the boat in the air like a duck's behind above water. Now they were looking down into the depths of the water, and staring into the vortex of a huge whirlpool.

'Yeaahhh!' yelled Jimbob as the boat slipped into the gaping opening. 'Ride 'er straight and true – no fearing now!'

And then with an enormous *whoosh* the boat *Pussin Water* slipped into the vortex like a tiny morsel entering a hungry mouth.

Then everything went quiet. The storm suddenly vanished and there was no more wind or rain. Everything was eerily quiet, and very, very dark. Sophie could neither see nor hear anything, as if floating in the vacuum of space. The only thing that let her know she was still in a physical space was the feeling of her hands gripped tightly upon the wheel. And yet she couldn't see the wheel, or even Jimbob who was standing right next to her.

'Where are we? What's going on? Jimbob, are you there?!' Sophie heard a low sniff and a snuffle.

'Ay, missy Sophie, Jimbob the Oldest Sproggit be 'ere. That was some whirly hole we just entered, eh?'

'Yeah, sure was. And what now?' Sophie was still stunned from the silence after the storm, and perplexed by the whole thing.

'Well, aye, it's a whirly-worm hole all right. And where it's taking us, nobody knows.'

'What?!'

'Aye, I mean, it's a whirly-worm hole, ain't it? These things can take us to anywhere…well, anywhere or nowhere inside the Imaginal World. Who knows, maybe they can even throw us out of it!'

'So we could end up miles from No-Place? I mean, even further away from No-Where.' Sophie could hear her own voice travel in the darkness like a lonesome ripple between stars.

'There be no miles here, missy Sophie. But don't ye worry – everything is connected, and nothing is not where it shouldn't be.'

Then the colors arrived. They came fast out of the darkest nowhere as if someone had thrown fireworks suddenly into the night sky. Streams of dazzling light came shooting past the ship, barely over their heads. Sophie's first thought was that they had entered into a blaze of shooting stars. The dashes of light whizzed past so fast that they soon turned into streaks. And then the streaks turned into lines; and the lines then became whole walls of light. The whole place lit up and the vastness of dark space instantly disappeared. Sophie could now see that they were in a huge tunnel, carved out from whooshing watery sides that tumbled around them. So this is what it's like to be in a whirly-worm hole, thought Sophie. The walls of colors streaking past soon disorientated Sophie and made her feel a little dizzy. It was lucky that she was still gripping the boat's wheel tightly as she wasn't prepared for what came next. The watery whirly-worm hole suddenly turned downward at an almost ninety-degree angle. The boat tipped its front end down again, and another *whoosh!* Then the tunnel turned sharply to the left…*whoosh!*…then up, and *whoosh!* Then to the right and *whoosh!* 'Ahhhh…! I'm gonna be sick!' Sophie could feel her stomach turning upon itself, just like the first time she had ridden a rollercoaster at the theme park. It was all she could do to keep grabbing onto the wheel as both the boat, and the wheel, was being whooshed around.

Sophie closed her eyes, as she knew that watching the lights was soon going to make her be sick. Again, she focused on moving into her tranquil inner space, where all was strong and quiet. She thought she could hear Jimbob speaking in a low voice. It sounded like Jimbob, although the tone was soft and gentle.

'Fear not, Sophie. Fear is the destroyer of worlds. Do not let fear enter into your thoughts or body – guard yourself.'

Sophie held onto her inner space, the place where she knew she could always find herself – even in the middle of a storm, or a whirly-worm hole. And in that place, all was quiet. Sophie could have been anywhere, in any world.

'Aye, missy Sophie, ye can open yer eyes now.'

When Sophie opened her eyes she was almost blinded by the light. A full, glaring daylight stung her and she had to immediately squint. Slowly, as her eyes became accustomed to the light, she saw that the boat was drifting softly upon a silent sea. Sophie was drenched to the skin, and her hands still gripped the wheel of the boat. She turned around and saw a very wet Jimbob grinning from wet-dogged ear to ear.

'Well, aye, we don't go through one of those every day. What would yer huffalot mates say about that one, eh?'

'Huff, probably.' Sophie tried to smile.

Jimbob strolled over to a wooden chest on the other side of the deck and opened it. Inside was full of empty pipes identical to the one he had been puffing on earlier. Picking up a pipe he popped it into his mouth and let out a long smokeless *puff*.

'Aye, that be better. Nothing like puffing on good sea air. What yer say to that, missy Sophie?'

Sophie laughed. 'I think you're an odd one, Jimbob. That's what I think!'

Jimbob smiled back and tipped his wet captain's cap. 'Aye, enough 'ave told me that, and I never said they weren't right.' He then looked ruefully over the boat and tutted. 'Ah, my poor *Pussin Water*. She sure ain't looking good. She's taken a real battering she 'as.'

Sophie looked at the broken sail mast, and all the rigging strewn over the floor of the lower deck. The boat was drifting now, having no source of power. She looked out at the great expanse of water, shimmering in innocence as if nothing had happened.

'Where are we, Jimbob?'

Jimbob the Oldest Sproggit rubbed his wet, brown fluffy-haired cheek with his pipe. 'Where is anywhere, Sophie?'

'I think we're lost, and maybe I'm never going to find No-Where or No-Place. It's always going to be far away – too far away.'

'I reckon, missy, that this No-Where of yours is as near or as far as it needs to be. And maybe this No-Place is in a different place for each person. Y'know, there ain't the same route for everyone.'

Sophie frowned. 'And why would that be? Is it not in one place?'

'Aye, missy Sophie, it be in one place – but *you* not be. Everyone needs their own journey, otherwise you won't arrive at the place when you're ready. And what use will you be then?'

'You make me feel even more lost Jimbob. I'm not sure if I should be listening to you!'

Sophie knew she didn't really mean that. She was becoming a little fond of the strange sea-wizened terrier captain, or last Sproggit, or whatever he was in this world!

Jimbob just shrugged. 'Well, you're only lost when you ain't listening right to yourself. Don't go blaming others now. Besides, a good sea captain is never lost.'

'How's that?'

'Cause there always be sea around. See what I mean?' Jimbob pointed out over the vast watery distance and chuckled.

'So, I guess that means we're still going in the right direction?'

'Aye, missy Sophie - in this world there is only one direction.'

And then Sophie knew, despite the appearances, that she was still on course for No-Where.

CHAPTER SIX – SNIFFLEGRUFF ISLAND

I cannot help you if you don't wake up

Being adrift on a boat with no means of navigation didn't seem so bad to Sophie. After all, there are worse situations to be in - such as stuck on the side of a dangerously high mountain with a fear of heights, or trapped in an underground tunnel with acute claustrophobia. As it was, drifting peacefully upon a lake-that-is-an-ocean was not at the top of the bad-situations-to-be-in-list; not even in the top five. And at least there were no more whirly-worm holes, or whatevers, plunging them through rollercoaster water tunnels. After that experience, all was pleasantly peaceful. Sophie no longer feared an unknown future, or what lay ahead of her. Jimbob also appeared to be enjoying the post-whirly-worm peace. He was strutting around the deck of the boat, inspecting the damage with occasional tut tuts, yet seemingly relaxed and smiling.

'Hey, missy, you were so serious back there in the storm.' Jimbob looked over at Sophie and grinned. 'Y'know, when you're all serious like that you can't see the connections. You only see the lines that run parallel and never join up. You gotta see the essential in all the mess. Then you know that nothing changes what's real – we just try to have fun putting the pieces together. So ponder not on that, missy Sophie, and laugh lighter, aye.'

'Aye, aye, Captain Jimbob,' replied Sophie with a salute.

The bright sky shone a hazy blue overhead and warmed Sophie until she was dry again. She went to sit down at the rear of the boat where Jimbob was stretched out relaxing. She too felt like she needed to spread out under the warmth of the day, and recharge her energies. Everything had happened so intensely since Sophie had first stepped through the door into this world. It was as if time was somehow speeded up and yet strangely absent simultaneously. Or rather, things did not pass according to time, yet to something else. It felt as if time was composed of events and experiences rather than of…well, of hours, minutes, and seconds. Maybe, she wondered, it was the experiences – of *having* the experiences – that processed time, and not the other way around.

'Jimbob, what exactly is the Imaginal World? I mean, this whole thing we're in now, if that makes any sense?'

Jimbob took the pipe out from his mouth and rubbed his soft, wet brown nose with it. 'Well, missy, it's kinda the place of all places, which 'as always been here…been 'ere long before your Regular World, that is. It's where ideas begin, before they trickle down to your dense realm. Everything 'ere is more fluid, more *real*. Ideas which are fixed, and don't change with your mind, they're less real. That's why your Regular World is heavier – everything is so fixed there. The Imaginal World floats around your world all the time, and yet no one notices. They see coincidences, and funny events, they do. Aye, but they can't see the lines that connect all these things together. The Regular World is like, well, so solid, and nobody pays much attention to the thoughts that drift into their minds.'

Jimbob sniffed, closed his eyes, and sat back.

Sophie wasn't sure if that made sense to her at all. 'But in our world,' she said, 'we make the thoughts. They don't drift into us, we make them!'

'Aye, that's what ye think. And that's what gets ye all into trouble.'

Trouble. There was that word again, and each time Sophie heard it she felt an ominous sensation in the pit of her stomach, as if a worm was wriggling about. Sophie was thinking about this when suddenly the boat shuddered, creaked, and then came to a stop. Jimbob opened one eye and looked about. The boat had run aground upon some rocks. Sophie eased herself up and looked over the side of the boat. They were indeed in shallow waters, and not far away was a beach – they had reached land! And for Sophie it looked exactly what she would imagine a desert island beach to look like, which was uncanny. They both quickly made their way ashore by wading through the shallow waters. Or rather, Sophie waded through whilst Jimbob doggie-paddled his way to shore. *See, I knew he was a dog!* Sophie thought to herself. When they arrived ashore they found the beach deserted, and ahead of them was nothing but forest.

'What do you think, Jimbob?' asked Sophie.

The captain nodded his old dogged head. 'I think something will turn up soon enough.'

'You think so?'

'Aye, it always does.'

Just then a tremor rippled under their feet as a *thud-thudding* could be heard coming closer. Sophie looked over at Jimbob, who just raised an eyebrow as if to say – aye, what next? Through a gap in the forest there appeared three large white hairy figures that came plodding towards them across the beach.

'It's a yeti!' Sophie said, astonished.

'A what? A year tea?'

'Nooo, the abominable snowman.'

Jimbob gave Sophie an odd look. 'A snowman, on a desert island? Are you cracker-mad, missy?'

The three large white hairy figures approached closer. Sophie breathed in deep and tried to remain calm, not giving in to fear. Seeing that Jimbob seemed not the least perturbed gave her some sense of ease. As the white hairy figures were only a short distance away she noticed that although covered in a shaggy white fur they each had a large ginger handlebar moustache.

Jimbob let out a long, low whistle. 'Aye, they be hairy hog-bears, missy Sophie. Nothing to worry about – they're just snifflegruffs.'

Sophie shook her head. 'Of course, snifflegruffs – what else!

SOPHIE'S SEARCH
FOR NO-WHERE

The three big white bear-yeti thingies came to a plodding halt before Sophie and Jimbob. They stood upright, and from their large height they peered down at the two new arrivals. Their faces, hog-like, had huge grinning mouths that contrasted with their snout noses. Sophie soon noticed that they each had a habit of sniffling whilst stroking their large ginger handlebar moustaches that curled around and connected with their sideburns. And then another strange sight hit her – they were all wearing black top hats! The whole effect was oddly comical. The three hog-bears took off their hats and, bowing slightly, introduced themselves as snifflegruffs before jabbing each other in the ribs. They appeared to be the friendliest hog-bears Sophie had ever met, or was ever likely to meet. Sophie and Jimbob accepted their invitation to stay with them, and followed them as they plod marched back into the forest. Strangely enough, as soon as they had entered the forest they exited it, the forest being about as dense as a cardboard cut out. And what they emerged into surprised Sophie totally – it was a whole city of snifflegruffs going about their snifflegruff business, all of then sniffling and wearing top hats. That, thought Sophie to herself, was definitely a first.

SOPHIE'S SEARCH
FOR NO-WHERE

As Sophie, Jimbob, and the three snifflegruffs marched through what appeared to be like a medieval city, all the other snifflegruffs waved, sniffled, stroked their ginger moustaches and hooted. Yes, they hooted – a kind of deep baritone chorus. With this almost classical baritone hooting, the stone-walled city, and the whole feel of the place, Sophie felt as if she had just stepped into a medieval play, like they put on at the theatre. Only that this theatre production had snifflegruffs instead of knights in armor. Sophie wasn't exactly sure which one out of the two she preferred. She looked over at Jimbob who likewise had an odd, curious 'what-the-jimbobs!' look on his fur-ruffled face. The walk – or rather parade – up to the city castle turned into a whole carnival. Snifflegruffs lined the narrow stone-cobbled streets and all threw their top hats in the air as the parade passed. All the snifflegruffs seemed to be cheering Sophie, and pointing to her and clapping. For Sophie, it all was beginning to feel a little disconcerting. Why was she so popular all of a sudden? After all, she was an unknown stranger…wasn't she? 'Just keep smiling – it's better than sniffling,' whispered Jimbob, somewhat ironically. There was little else Sophie could do anyway.

Shortly they were led into the castle and finally into a great hall. At the end of the hall stood a lavish throne that was finely ornamented and draped in bright textures. The snifflegruffs led Sophie and Jimbob to the throne then all three of them took off their top hats, sniffled, twisted their golden moustaches, and bowed.

'Here, we meet our ruler. I am Jedly, spokesgruff of the snifflegruffs,' said the leading snifflegruff. The other two snifflegruffs nodded in agreement, and grinned widely.

'Pleased to meet you, I am Sophie,' replied Sophie with a pleasant smile.

'Aye, Jimbob the Oldest Sproggit at yer service.'

A moment of silence turned into a longer moment of silence, which finally twisted into an uncomfortable moment of silence. Everyone was looking at each other and smiling. The snifflegruffs were simultaneously smiling widely and sniffle-stroking (as Sophie came to call their habit of sniffling and stroking their moustaches).

'Well, is your ruler not coming?' Sophie did not feel as if she wanted to waste any more time. She had a quest to complete, and she was in no mind, or mood, to forget that. The three snifflegruffs burst into fits of sniffle-stroking and giggles.

'Well?' repeated Sophie.

Jedly stepped forward, still giggling, with his top hat now back on his furry white head and wiggling.

'It's you Sophie!' he said pointing directly at her. 'You're the queen of Snifflegruff City now!' As he said that a great horn was blown, a sound which blasted out from the castle windows over the city. A huge hooting rose up from the streets below.

'No, I can't! It's not right!' protested Sophie.

Yet the snifflegruffs were adamant that Sophie was to be their next ruler, and the great fuss, fanfare, and outright kafuffle had already begun.

In less than a horse-hair slither of time Sophie was promptly declared ruler of Snifflegruff City, and presented with a black top hat of her own – which she was advised to wear for official occasions. Then the life of royalty began, without wasting any more precious seconds. Sophie was literally being whooshed along with events so quickly that any protests from her just fell flat, or were quashed by amiable sniffle-stroking.

SOPHIE'S SEARCH
FOR NO-WHERE

As part of her triumphant and rapid rise to power (she had no challengers), Sophie was obliged to visit many snifflegruff establishments – merchants, important monuments, etc – and to royally announce the snifflegruff sacred holidays, for which there were many, apparently! And that was how it all began. Soon Sophie's days became full of ruler responsibilities and little else. Her snifflegruff private guard escorted Sophie all over the city, treating her royally and respectfully. She didn't need a guard to protect her, since all the snifflegruffs were most welcoming and over-zealous in friendliness. Her guards were there to make sure she could escape in time to make the next important snifflegruff appointment. And throughout all this Sophie was adorned with luxuries and comfort she was unaccustomed to. Yet the one thing she did regret was the absence of her friend Jimbob. The oldest Sproggit had shortly taken his leave and asked for supplies to repair his boat. The last Sophie had seen of him was the morning he left for the coast with a line of snifflegruffs carrying wood and tools. She had desperately wanted to go and visit him yet her new found friend – Jedly the spokesgruff – stuck to her like hair gel and always kept her busy. The days just seemed to pass so quickly, one after the other.

SOPHIE'S SEARCH
FOR NO-WHERE

At first Sophie had felt great frustration at having her plans thwarted

by the cute insanity of the snifflegruffs and their city life. She was also

greatly frustrated that she was wasting time in finding No-Place and

getting to No-Where. Yet there was an enduring sense of something

highly agreeable about being with the snifflegruffs. After a while

Sophie came to realize that this feeling of agreeableness was the sense

of 'being loved.' And after all, who doesn't want to be loved? Amongst

the affable, warm, and sociable snifflegruffs Sophie felt wanted – and

needed. And this sense of being loved kept Sophie in Snifflegruff City,

and upon the island…and further away from where she really needed

to be. And the more Sophie sensed this warm feeling inside of her

from the attention and affection of the snifflegruffs, the more they

piled it on. In short, the whole of the city adored Sophie. They

worshipped the cobblestones her dainty feet walked upon. The male

snifflegruffs, the female snifflegruffs, the baby snifflegruffs – even the

elderly snifflegruffs – all smothered Sophie with as much hog-bear

affection as was possible. In time Sophie no longer wondered what it

was they really wanted from her. She was just content enough that the

snifflegruffs liked her, and wanted her around. It was also an extra

bonus that being a tropical island the climate was almost perfect for

SOPHIE'S SEARCH
FOR NO-WHERE

Sophie – warm sun all of the days. Around the city too there were many grassy areas surrounded by high palm-like trees that gave shade, where Sophie loved to visit. And you could be sure that whenever she visited these grassy areas several baby snifflegruffs also came out to play. Sophie had great fun throwing the baby snifflegruffs around like fluffy snowballs that rolled on the grass and then sprang back to life, sniffling and bouncing on their strong hog-bear feet. The days of warmth and fun were like a dream come true…only that Sophie didn't consider it to be a dream. And that became the problem…and soon she even forgot that she was in the Imaginal World, or that the Imaginal World existed at all - whatever it was.

The reality of Snifflegruff Island and its snifflegruff medieval city soon became her only sense of reality. It was as if the white snifflegruff hog-bear fluff had infiltrated into her mind, fluffing it up entirely! Sophie thought no more about her quest, about finding No-Where, or even being away from her home in the Regular World. The inner quiet part of her which guided Sophie when she really needed it had been sniffle-silenced and muffled. She was now Queen Sophie – Ruler of Snifflegruff City and of the whole island – and going nowhere. Sophie's private entourage grew and grew. Everywhere she went she was accompanied by a long line of snifflegruffs at her service, fluffing at her every need.

Then one day, unexpectedly, an odd niggling feeling entered Sophie's mind.

'Jedly?'

'Yes, Sophie, m'lady.' Jedly the spokesgruff, now the queen's top hog-bear, sniffled as he spoke.

'I haven't been to the ocean for such a long time. I think it's about time I saw it again.'

Jedly sniffle-stroked his moustache and shook his large hairy white head. 'I don't think that would be best for you, my dear Queen. It's so far away, and your feet are so daintily small. The two just don't go together – it's like hog marmalade and nut-paste, they just don't go!'

'I've had enough of your hog marmalade to last me a thousand snifflegruff moons! But I just have an urge, a feeling, to visit the ocean. And I just feel that I must go soon.' Sophie began walking out of the city and toward the slither-thin forest that surrounded it. Jedly looked at the other snifflegruffs who all had the same worried hog-bear look on their faces. He then hog-hopped in front of Sophie and spread his arms wide.

'Sophie, dearest Queen. The ocean is no place for such a delicate lady. There is salt in the water and it may corrode your skin. Nay, let us return to the city and visit one of our parks. You can play with the little snifflegruffs. They adore you so much!' Jedly sniffle-stroked and did his best to smile.

'And I adore them too. Yet today is ocean day. I can feel it pulling inside of me. Now step aside Jedly or I shall pull on your ginger moustache!'

Jedly frowned and stepped aside. Sophie marched out of the city walls and towards the beach where, unknowingly, she had first arrived with Jimbob many moons ago. Yet somehow Sophie had already forgotten this, her memory having been smothered by snifflegruff fluff. Despite her forgetfulness, Sophie still felt a tugging feeling deep within her, as though she was missing something, or had misplaced something. Although she couldn't put her finger on it she knew that there was something amiss, some disconnect that wasn't quite right. And within that odd space inside of her a feeling of the ocean tugged at Sophie.

SOPHIE'S SEARCH
FOR NO-WHERE

The entourage of snifflegruffs edged uneasily behind Sophie as she passed through the forest wall and onto the beach. Some way in the distance she saw the outline of a boat anchored in the water, and a small figure standing near to it on the sand. Curious, Sophie walked over toward the small, dark figure.

'Don't go Queeny, it could be dangerous.' Jedly hopped uneasily from one hog-bear foot to the other. His usual snifflegruff face-wide smile was now a semi-grimace.

'Yes, Queen Sophie, don't go!' A chorus of voices and sniffles rose from the entourage behind her.

Sophie was not deterred. 'If it's dangerous, then I have my dear snifflegruffs to protect me, don't I?'

The line of snifflegruffs looked at each other and politely nodded. Jedly rolled his eyes, and his black top hat slid to one side of his head.

'We cannot stop you in anything you wish to do, Queen Sophie. That is the law of Snifflegruff Island during your reign as Queen. Everything you do must be your choice, and so too are the consequences of your decisions.' Jedly bowed and tipped his top hat.

Sophie approached close to what appeared to be a small furry-brown dog-like creature in ship uniform.

'Queen Sophie, missy, your boat is now ready to leave…aye, it is.' The small doggy creature tipped his captain's hat, yet stared firmly into Sophie's eyes.

'My boat?' said Sophie, somewhat puzzled. 'Since when did I have a boat?'

'Since you started on your quest to find your…y'know, your special No-Where, missy Sophie.'

Sophie shook her head. 'My special nowhere? Why would I want to go nowhere? Surely I'd want to go somewhere, wouldn't I?'

The dog-eared sea-weary creature that was Jimbob the Oldest Sproggit gave a sorrowful shake of his head. He looked over to the snifflegruffs who were now grinning and seeming more at ease.

'Aye, I'm sorry Sophie but I can't interfere more than this. Everything in this world must come from you. I cannot help you if you don't wake up.'

'Wake up? But I'm already awake. Why would I want to wake up again if I'm awake now?' said Sophie a little puzzled.

'Aye, there are dreams within dreams, missy. And within dreams begin responsibilities. You will know when you know. Until then…'

The scrawny fellow that was Jimbob the Oldest Sproggit gave a bow and moved away.

An unusual feeling stirred within Sophie, as if something known to her was tapping away from the inside. There was a thread of some knowing within that she could not connect with, nor understand its presence. Suddenly, a chorus of snifflegruff hoots and sniffles shook Sophie out of her reverie. Jedly shuffled up and nudged her with his large hog-bear elbow.

'Come on Queen Sophie, we must be going. There are all the snifflegruffs in the city who need you. They all love you in the city. You want to be loved, don't you, Queenie?'

'Yes…yes, I guess I do,' replied Sophie softly, lost in some clouded thought.

Jedly hooted and sniffle-stroked in pleasure, whilst all the other snifflegruffs in the entourage cheer-sniffled. They escorted Sophie back along the beach, through the thin slither of forest, and back to Snifflegruff City where comfort was once again bestowed upon Sophie. For the rest of the day she had fun playing with the excitable little baby snifflegruffs who chased her around the park, throwing freshly plucked hog-bear fluff balls.

SOPHIE'S SEARCH
FOR NO-WHERE

Later that evening Sophie sat alone in her private royal chamber, staring out of the window upon the star-sprinkled sky. Out there in the distance somewhere there was a destination waiting for her. She couldn't say how or why she knew this; it was just some feeling inside. Then the door to her chamber opened and one of the snifflegruff female attendants entered. Sophie knew this female snifflegruff well and she was one of her favorites. Her name was Fiffy, and yet her hog-bear fur was so fluffy that Sophie preferred to call her Fluffy to tease her. She called Fluffy over. The female attendant came to her and made an awkward snifflegruff bow by taking off her top hat.

'Fluffy, do you know anything about a special place? Maybe it's somewhere near here?'

'Ooh, a special place you say? Isn't everywhere special? But I can't say that I know about these things – if you know what I mean?' The female snifflegruff rolled her eyes and made a conspicuous sniffle-stroke.

'No, I don't think I do know what you mean. Is there a meaning to that which I don't know what you mean?'

Fluffy sniffle-stroked again, and then a second time. 'Is it a special place in particular – a big or a small place? Special places can be many sizes can't they, my Queen?'

'Fluffy, stop beating around the bush!'

'Ah, so its bushes now you're talking about. There are lots of bushes in our city.'

'No!' Sophie had raised her voice unexpectedly, making the snifflegruff nervously step back. 'I'm sorry Fluffy, I didn't mean to startle you.'

'It's Fiffy,' the snifflegruff replied coyly.

'Okay, Fiffy. I'm sorry. It's just that I'm interested to know if there's a special place near here.'

'There's no-place no-where near here...oops!' Fiffy suddenly covered her mouth with her hog-bear hand. 'I mean...what I mean is that there are no special places nowhere here on this island.'

Sophie caught a sense of something. 'Okay, so if there is no special place nowhere on this island, then where is it?' The snifflegruff sniffle-stroked and then looked away from Sophie, trying to avoid eye contact.

'Well, Fiffy? Come on, how long have we known each other?'

Fiffy cocked her head as if thinking. 'Well, that be about almost one snifflegruff year. Oh my!'

Saying that, the snifflegruff gave out an odd shriek-like hoot and hog-marched out of the room, leaving Sophie confused.

Almost one snifflegruff year? Sophie said to herself. That cannot be, it's only been days, not a year!

SOPHIE'S SEARCH
FOR NO-WHERE

Sophie began to feel increasingly uneasy over the coming days as the sense of something-not-quite-right began to grow stronger within her. She would still play with the baby snifflegruffs on the grass, visit the parks, and stroll around the cheerful city. All city life appeared as normal, with the daily snifflegruff markets a joyful, noisy, and often crazy event with all the stallholders hooting and trying to attract their customers. On one occasion she even managed to escape from her escort and head down to the beach to see if she could talk with that odd scrawny sea captain fellow again – yet neither he nor his boat was there.

'What am I a queen of?' Sophie spoke out aloud to herself. She knew that despite all the comfort, the adoration, and the privileges, that she was still unfulfilled. There was one thing that she felt was now desperately missing…if only she could put her finger on it…

'Destiny, that's it!' said Sophie out loud. 'I'm missing my destiny.'

For the rest of the day the atmosphere around Snifflegruff City seemed oddly different, as if expectant of something. The snifflegruffs in the street appeared a little sadder, thought Sophie. They seemed a little

edgy too, and were not as forthcoming as usual in their friendliness. Or

was Sophie only imagining this? Was it, she wondered, just the result of

her own preoccupations and distracted mind? The feeling of missing

her destiny had begun to grow stronger within Sophie now and was

beginning to gnaw at her. The whole day had suddenly changed into an

unpleasant sensation that felt out of sorts. The previous days of fun

and frolics now appeared hollow and empty. Was this it?

Sophie marched to the castle where she had her luxurious quarters,

with her two snifflegruff escorts following dutifully behind.

'Hey, you don't always have to follow me, you know. I'm okay. No

snifflegruff is going to kidnap me. The worst that could happen is that

I could get lost. Why don't you just leave me alone?'

The two snifflegruffs escorting Sophie just sniffle-stroked and looked

around as if they hadn't heard her.

'Dah, forget it!' Sophie entered through the main door of the castle and

went to look for Jedly, her main snifflegruff when she needed answers.

She found Jedly polishing the royal horn in the throne room.

'Getting ready to make an announcement?' she asked.

Jedly sniffle-stroked and his hog-bear eyes lit up. 'There are always reasons to celebrate in Snifflegruff City! Everything comes to pass here.'

'And how did things come to pass here before I arrived, before you had a queen?' Sophie moved closer to Jedly, observing his regular slow rhythm and seeming nonchalance.

Jedly shrugged. 'Sometimes we are without a ruler. Then we snifflegruffs are sad. We like our rulers - we like you.'

'Then there were others before me? Other queens? Other rulers? You mean I'm not the first?' For the first time Sophie had ignored a snifflegruff compliment.

'You're not the first, nor the last. We like each of you. Your time with us is always special. We snifflegruffs love each of you...for your time.' Jedly straightened up and walked over to where he placed the royal horn on its rack. 'We have really loved you, Sophie. You have been a good ruler for us. Now it is very soon your time.' Then Jedly left the room without another word.

Other rulers?

Each loved in their time?

Soon my time?

SOPHIE'S SEARCH
FOR NO-WHERE

Things were not making much sense to Sophie, and that nagging sensation from before tightened within her gut. She decided to make her way to one of the castle's towers, which was a favorite spot of hers.

Looking out from the high window of the tower Sophie gazed over the whole of the island, and far away to the horizon of the sea. For the first time since her arrival, so many days before - was it days? - Sophie yearned for travel, for movement. Yet to where she did not know; only that she felt a longing for movement toward *something*. It was then she heard a voice speak –

'Keep your intention before you at every step you take. You wish for freedom, and you must never forget it.'

Sophie quickly turned around and saw a figure standing in the frame of the doorway to the tower. She stepped back in surprise, thinking she was alone. Composing herself, she realized that the figure - a man all dressed in green - was somehow familiar to her.

'Who are you?' she asked, still a little startled.

'How are *you*?' the figure in green replied. When Sophie did not reply the figure spoke again: 'Without will and intention we do not have sufficient force to embrace destiny. We remain in the arms of fate that push us around with false needs and desires. You must regain your own strength of personal will and intention.'

The figure swiftly turned around and left before Sophie had time to think of what to say. She ran to the open doorway and looked down the steps that lead away, yet there was no sight of the mysterious figure. A slight apprehension arose within her. Sophie ran down the stairs and to her own private quarters. As she flung open the door and entered her room she suddenly sensed something was different.

Her room was bare of all her personal items - the gifts that had been bestowed upon her, memorabilia from the city, and items collected from royal visits. All was gone. The room looked bare and empty without their personal presence. It was then that Sophie heard the royal horn blow.

'A royal announcement…without me knowing?'

She quickly ran over to her large bedroom window and gazed down over the city streets. Sophie saw that all the snifflegruffs had gathered below the castle and were standing still, their large mustachioed hog-bear heads hung low. Something strange was happening, or about to happen, and Sophie needed to know what it was. She ran from her room and through the castle corridors toward the throne room, from where the horn must have been blown. As she burst into the throne room she saw Jedly standing in the centre, also looking sad. Sophie stepped toward him and almost jumped as the doors loudly slammed shut behind her. Her way out was blocked by two of the large security snifflegruffs, who both looked at her without expression.

'We thank you for coming, Queen Sophie. It is with regret that we inform you your reign is finished. A snifflegruff year has passed and yet you are still with us. We must remove you now.'

Jedly gave a loud sniffle-stroke, and all the other snifflegruffs in the room followed. The chorus of sniffles echoed throughout the room, and ended on a low, deep sniffle.

'One year?! It can't be! I haven't been here that long. What do you mean?' protested Sophie.

Jedly stepped forward toward her. 'It is the law in Snifflegruff City. After one snifflegruff year the guest ruler must be removed. It is the only way to maintain stability, and to avoid the trappings of power. If the ruler has not chosen to abdicate within the given time, then they forfeit their right to leave freely. One year of our time has now passed. We must now remove you to your next place of stay.'

'Next place of stay?' asked Sophie nervously, as if not wishing to know the answer.

Jedly bowed solemnly. 'Yes, my ex-Queen. We must place you in exile, away from our island. You must pass through Decision Hall.'

The two strong snifflegruffs standing behind Sophie grabbed her and pulled her away. Sophie screamed and tried to struggle, yet to no avail. She was held tight by the grip of the snifflegruffs.

CHAPTER SEVEN – UNDER A BLOOD-RED MOON

You can always find a way when you believe you can do amazing things

Against her wishes Sophie had been taken from the castle and placed into a caged carriage. Four somber snifflegruffs, with their top hats perched sturdily, pulled the carriage through the narrow streets of the city. From within the locked cage Sophie watched in great sadness as she passed the snifflegruffs that lined the streets. As the carriage passed, the snifflegruffs all took off their top hats and hung their heads. This time there was no hooting, no smiling and pointing, no celebration or joy; only sadness in the air that spread like a contagion. After all the adoration and attention that Sophie had received from the snifflegruffs who, it had to be admitted, had been wonderful hosts, it now seemed an impossible nightmare that they would do this to her. The sudden switch from being beloved queen to some kind of caged prisoner seemed so oddly unreal to Sophie that she was not sure it was really happening. Her mind was a frantic blur. The high stone walls of the city streets now loomed over Sophie as the carriage hobbled along. The whole atmosphere had turned oppressive, and the once-friendly snifflegruffs were now her apologetic jailers. How had it come to this?

SOPHIE'S SEARCH
FOR NO-WHERE

What was it she had done wrong - or rather, had not done right? Had she been expected to walk away from being queen before the snifflegruff year was over? Yet it hadn't been that long…how was she to know!

With her head full of thoughts, Sophie barely recognized that the carriage was being pulled toward a large domed building at the far edge of the city. It was a building Sophie had never visited before, nor had she even known of its existence. It stood at the far edge, where the city dropped away to nowhere. As the carriage approached closer she saw that it was an oddly shaped building, neither round nor square. Soon the solemn snifflegruff procession halted before the strange building's large door. It was then that Sophie realized the building had no windows, and stood like a spaceship of stone.

Jedly bowed before Sophie as she was taken down from the carriage. 'Sophie, we have arrived at Decision Hall, where your exile begins. It is with sadness that we must say our farewells. Snifflegruff City has enjoyed your presence. Yet all things must pass, and this too shall pass. We have our ways here, which have their function. Everything is for its time and place. You must leave us now. Inside of this building you will find eight doors. When you feel it is time, make your choice and move through one of the doors. There is no coming back, and no leaving the building. May your fate be good to you.'

Before Sophie could even muster a reply she was lifted by the two snifflegruff guards and taken through the main portal of the building. Then she felt the arms holding her release their grip, and heard the sound of a large, solid door closing behind her.

A soft illumination filled the large interior room, revealing a domed ceiling. In the middle of the room was a rug with cushions. There were no windows, nor any light source, and Sophie was unable to see from where the soft glow came from. Yet the atmosphere was somehow soothing, and in total contrast to the oddness outside. Sophie sat down on the cushions and closed her eyes. She breathed slowly and deeply, wishing to find a space of peace where she could think. With each breath she took her mind began to clear, as if some fluff cloud was slowly lifting from her. Gradually the images from her journey began to unfold and re-emerge into her memory. After a short while of sitting quietly on the cushions Sophie could remember everything, including all that had happened before landing on the island of the snifflegruffs.

'Oh, Jimbob, what have I done? How could I have not recognized you! My quest…oh, I've been so stupid. You silly Sophie, you got yourself distracted with those damn fluffy hog-bears. Never again!' It was then that Sophie also remembered the words of the Green Man in the castle tower: 'Without will and intention we do not have sufficient force to embrace destiny. We remain in the arms of fate that push us around with false needs and desires. You must regain your own strength of personal will and intention.'

Sophie opened her eyes, and for the first time in a long time she saw things clearly. Even in this world we can get easily distracted, she thought…*Worlds within worlds - As it is in the Regular World so it is here too…* Sophie muttered quietly under her breath. She knew she had to make a decision, a choice - any choice. The alternative, which was doing nothing, was the worst thing to do. Jedly, in his parting words, had wished that her fate be good to her.

'It's not fate that I'm interested in - it's destiny,' whispered Sophie into the emptiness before her.

SOPHIE'S SEARCH
FOR NO-WHERE

Sophie stood up and observed closely the large domed room. It had eight walls, and in each of the eight walls was a door - eight doors to choose from. In soft steps Sophie walked the circumference of the room, slowly passing from one door to the next. As she came to each door she paused, closed her eyes, breathed deeply, and listened... listened quietly to that place deep inside. Sophie was listening for the faint wisps of destiny that blow through our lives. Sometimes we can hear these faint wisps in our dreams, or sometimes in the midst of our everyday lives. They are always around, fleeting, scratching against the back of our minds.

After visiting all eight doors she returned to her cushions and sat down again and closed her eyes. A very slight and subtle change had entered into Sophie, and nestled within her. It felt like a connection - a connection to something larger than herself. It was just a feeling, a sense; intangible and unknown. Yet it drew her forward, as if a silver cord were pulling her. Sophie opened her eyes, stood up, and walked towards one of the unmarked doors. She opened it and stepped through...

...into complete darkness...

…Then shadows formed as a blood red moon rose over the horizon. As Sophie's eyes adjusted to the dim light she could make out a wasteland lit by a low red glow that crept over the landscape like a hunter. Sophie's body gave a shiver; not with cold, for it was not, but because of an eerie energy that was present. Then she saw it: in the distance a tall tower that shimmered luminous green. It stood like a giant missile, pointing upwards into the blood-red night sky. Sophie's stomach tightened as she sensed some sinister force. Looking around her immediate vicinity she noticed the outline of a large mansion, now in fallen ruins. It was the nearest building to her, and her only shelter. Approaching the ruins over rocky ground she soon came upon a large sign stuck over the entrance. Upon it was written: '***One must come here by neither foot nor transport - and speak to me neither indoors nor out. If this person comes, there is hope. If not, then all is lost.***' Sophie read the sign a second time, then closed her eyes to listen…to listen to the connection inside. Then she knew what to do.

Sophie lay herself down across the threshold of the entrance to the ruined mansion, her body half in, half out. In a calm, clear voice she called out, 'I arrived here by a doorway, from another land. I neither came by foot nor transport. I am neither in nor out now, as I speak to you. I have fulfilled all your requests.' Sophie lay still upon the ground, hearing the throb of her own heartbeat. Then she heard the sound of movement from not too far away, of feet treading over loose stones.

'Come in, stranger. You are welcome to enter.' The voice was that of a man, and sounded old and tired.

Sophie got up and carefully stepped into the ruined building, guided only by the dim haze of a moon-reddened night sky.

'Come, come, whoever you are. Be not afraid. I bid you welcome. Here, follow my voice.'

Sophie followed from where the voice came from, and saw some steps leading down toward a flicker of light.

'Is anyone down there?' Sophie felt a little hesitant to venture down into the unknown. The whole place seemed to vibrate with an eerie energy that made her feel uncomfortable.

'Yes. There is only myself. You must come down here, it will be safer.' The man's voice sounded soft, and gentle, and so Sophie made the decision to follow it down the steps. From the haze of the blood-red moon above, and a flicker of light from below, Sophie could see enough to tread carefully down each step. When she reached the bottom she found herself in a low-roofed room, lit by candles. A large, rounded figure scuffled forward from the darkness of the far corner. Sophie saw that it was an old man covered in layers of rags. As the figure entered the light of the candles she stepped back and drew breath. The old man looked at her from eyes set in a deeply scarred face. It was a face so different from the soft voice she had heard calling to her.

'Do not look at my outward shape, but take what is in my hand.' The scarred figure opened his hands and within was a tiny bird with bright yellow feathers and longish red legs. The tiny bird chirped sweetly, then flew out of the man's hands and perched on an alcove in the wall.

'What is this place? And who are you?' Sophie was more bewildered than she had been in a long time.

The old man, who seemed frail despite his large size, crouched in the middle of the room beside the candles. Sophie now saw that the old man was bald, and had a hairless face. Yet his face was taut as if unnaturally stretched before its years.

'You have many questions, and not all of them I can answer. Yet I will try.'

Sophie, now feeling more comfortable in the presence of the old man, approached the middle of the room. She looked into the man's eyes, and saw that despite the mutilation of his face, he had kind eyes.

The man coughed. 'My name is Ralph, and this is my home. This used to be a beautiful place. This building was a monastery, and I've served here almost all my life. Now it is in ruins, and a dark energy has entered this land. This dark energy rules over everything.'

'What happened?'

'I know from where you have come,' said Ralph. 'You are another visitor from the Regular World, like the one before you. And your world is responsible for what is happening here. Something entered this part of our world from your Regular World. There were some terrible dark thought-forms that erupted suddenly in your world. They must have originated in one particular spot – a place that corresponds with our land here. We felt the burst of these thought-forms as screams of pain, anger, confusion, and worst of all – hatred. The energy of hatred and revenge ripped into our world, shaking the very foundations. Our monastery here collapsed in ruins, and many of us here were injured. We suspect it probably reflected a similar collapse of one of your great buildings in the Regular World. You see, everything is connected. Just because you don't see something, doesn't mean that it doesn't exist.'

Ralph sighed and touched his face.

SOPHIE'S SEARCH
FOR NO-WHERE

'All my brothers of the monastery left this place, in the hope of keeping our teachings alive and transmitting them elsewhere. I had to stay behind. It was my duty as Abbott of the monastery. Besides, I was myself already damaged from the event, and could be hurt no further.'

A deep sadness entered into Sophie's heart. 'You said a dark energy has entered this place. What do you mean?' she asked.

'What I mean is that the angry thought-forms from your world created a monster in ours. That was when the ghoul appeared, and terrorized this place. The energy of fear reigns here now. My own fear is that a rip between our two worlds has now been created which could threaten to spread across the Imaginal World.' Ralph shook his head wearily.

'You said that someone else had come before?'

'Yes, someone like you, from the Regular World.'

'And? Where are they now?'

'Did you see that tall green monstrosity of a tower when you were above?'

Sophie nodded her head.

'Well, they are in that tower somewhere, and a prisoner of the horrible ghoul.' Ralph's voice sounded weak and tired.

SOPHIE'S SEARCH
FOR NO-WHERE

Sophie sat back and quietly observed the flickering of the candlelight.
The situation didn't sound good. It was a dark, oppressive world that
she was in. Yet why had she chosen this world? What force within her
had compelled her to choose *that* door to come here? Sophie had
enough sense to realize that things do not happen without rhyme or
reason – least of all in the Imaginal World! Cause and effect do not
often occur in straight lines, as we imagine them to, but causes *do* have
their effects somewhere down the line.

'I know I must be here for a reason,' said Sophie out loud. 'I know that
in this world I have my destiny to follow. It's a choice I've made to do
my *one thing*.' Sophie's voice sounded determined.
Ralph looked deeply into her eyes and the iris of his own eyes seemed
to wink at her.
'Well, you did solve the first riddle, unlike your previous compatriot.
That's a good start. That was a riddle I put there to counteract the
ghoul's curse that keeps people away from entering this place.' Ralph
wagged his finger at Sophie. 'Yet there are more riddles. And with
these riddles the obnoxious ghoul keeps me prisoner in this forsaken
ruin, unable to leave. Each day he comes to taunt me, and asks me
these riddles. And each day I must suffer his torment and humiliation.'

'Tell them to me, and I will help you.'

Ralph told Sophie the three riddles of his imprisonment. The both of them then sat in silence, shadows flickering on the walls around them. It felt to Sophie as if she was in some deep cave, blocked off from the world.

Suddenly a great rumble and roar could be heard around the building. Sophie thought that everything above was about to collapse on top of her. A low gurgling sound then echoed through the room, like the sound of water drowning in water.

'It's him – *that creature!*' Ralph moaned. 'It's time to face him…again.'

The large old man slowly hobbled up the steps and out into the dark night of the blood-reddened moon. Sophie followed apprehensively. As they approached the threshold of the ruined monastery they saw the nauseous creature, roaring and hopping in delight. At first it was strange to make out just what type of creature he was. It was all skin and bone, covered by a single loin cloth. Its hands were long and spindly, like flesh spikes. Red eyes glowed from within deep eye sockets, and where the nose should have been was a hole flimsily covered by a flap of dead hanging skin. His head was covered by long strands of greasy black hair in patches. The ghoul looked like the walking dead itself. It roared, cursed, and mocked.

'You still alive, you miserable old monk? You should have rotted away long ago. You smell of dead meat already, ha!' The creature delighted in taunting and mocking the old man. 'I should have gnawed on your bones the first time I saw you.' Then the ghoul noticed Sophie, who was standing behind Ralph, a little way back. 'Ah, another visitor you have here. Tasty! Your friend will be coming with me just like the last one. Tasty and ohh…nice, nice!' The ghoul stuck out its tongue and several worms fell out of its mouth.

'We are only your prisoners if we cannot answer your riddles,' called out Ralph weakly.

'Bah! You've never been able to answer my riddles, you feeble old wretch. You will rot away before you can give me my answers.'

'Maybe so, or maybe not.' Ralph picked up a stone and threw it at the creature.

The ghoul leaped forward onto the crumbling wall, and sat there hunched upon its squat feet. 'Hah, you miserable old fool!' I'll riddle you again, before I taunt you - old man and little, tasty girl.'

SOPHIE'S SEARCH
FOR NO-WHERE

Sophie stepped forward. 'Riddle us then, and get on with it.'

The ghoul spat upon the ground. 'Tell me, fateful wanderer - how many stars are in the sky?'

Sophie paused. 'There are as many stars as there are souls in all of the worlds.' Then she smiled and added – 'and as many stars as hairs on a ghoul's head. If you don't believe it's true, then for each hair you pluck out I will tell you the name of that star.' The ghoul gurgled and spat on the ground. 'Bah…right, first time, you impudent wretch! Now, second riddle - how far is it from here to the end of the world?'

'That's easy. It's just as far as the return journey from the end of the world to here.'

Again the ghoul gurgled and spat. 'Grrh, right again! But now you must answer me this - when will the moon disappear?'

'The moon will disappear when everyone stops believing in it.'

The ghoul let out an almighty shriek and fell back from the wall.

'Trickery, what trickery is this! Ah, damn you, wanderer!' And with a piercing wail it scampered away from the ruined monastery toward its green tower. The darkened sky seemed to shudder and shake.

SOPHIE'S SEARCH
FOR NO-WHERE

Ralph leaned upon Sophie for balance. 'You have done well, young girl. You show great promise. Now tell me, *who* are you and how exactly did you come to be here?'

Sophie breathed in deeply. It was time to tell her story again.

'My name is Sophie, and I came here from what you call the Regular World to seek out No-Where, which is at No-Place. But I think it's going to be much harder than I first thought. I'm not sure exactly how I came to be here, in this place. Each step I take leads me somewhere completely different. I don't think I'm making any progress. I'm not sure if I'll ever find my way to No-Where. Everything just seems like a maze, so scrambled, so odd. It's so absurd that I can't make any sense of it.' Sophie looked at Ralph and she could sense that behind his scarred face he had a soft heart.

'You can always find a way when you believe you can do amazing things. You know, Sophie, things may appear chaotic or absurd here in the Imaginal World yet everything has its own rules and ways of operating. In this place, there are functions behind appearances. But your Regular World works with externals and less so with the meanings and significances behind them. Follow your intention, and trust your intuition, my girl.'

'And will my intuition lead me to where I need to go?'

Ralph smiled and nodded. 'If you are connected, Sophie, then your intuition will tell you everything.'

'But back home, I couldn't make sense of the world.' Sophie shrugged. 'I always thought the answers lay somewhere else, outside of my own world. Maybe that's why I wanted so badly to come here.'

'Many of the experiences you have in the Regular World are signs to a greater truth. They are only the indicators, and not the final destination. Everything that happens in your Regular World has a greater reality here in the Imaginal World. This world compliments your own, and makes you whole and complete. Here is where your dreams begin.'

'And where do they end?'

'I hope they never end, otherwise we'd be in trouble then!' Ralph laughed, which soon turned into coughing.

The two figures, the frail old man and Sophie, sat close to the candles in the centre of the basement room. It was not for heat that they sat close to the candles, for the atmosphere was strangely humid and warm. It was for the light, for it gave them a remembrance of a world away from darkness and a blood-red moon. Ralph told Sophie stories of his days as the Head Abbott at the monastery, and the jokes they played on each other.

'I thought all monks were serious!' said Sophie with a chuckle.

'Ah, only about as far as you can throw them' replied Ralph, as he wrapped his torn rags around his body.

'And how long have you been here alone?'

Ralph peered over at Sophie in the semi-illuminated darkness. 'I have been here many blood-red moons, yet I have not been here alone.'

'You mean there are others here?' Sophie looked surprised.

'What I mean, dear girl, is that I am connected at all times. Here in the Imaginal World everything is connected, if we only open ourselves to it. It is the same in your world, only that it is harder because the Regular World is so dense, and the connections less detectable.' Ralph paused. 'But, yes, there is another - the one who came before you, as I said. The ghoul took him because he could not answer his riddles.'

'And where is he now? Who is he?'

'As I told you, no doubt he is within the ghoul's tower, and probably chained in a tiny room as we speak. Who he is…well, he was a wanderer like you, one of those from your world. And similar age to you I reckon.'

Ralph went over to an old wooden chest and pulled out some blankets, which he gave to Sophie. 'These don't have holes in, like mine. I reserve them for guests.' He smiled.

'And where do we go from here then?' asked Sophie, as she spread out her blanket on the floor.

'That's a very lazy question, Sophie. I've heard it used so many times. You should be asking yourself, where do *I* go from here.'

Sophie sat quietly for a while, deep in thought, trying to connect again with that place inside of her. It was some time before she spoke again. 'My sense is that I need to try to rescue this other person, this wanderer like me, as you say. Yet everything here is connected with that ghoul. He must be dealt with first. Is there any way I can get around this ghoul?'

Ralph nodded his head slowly. 'You are right. Everything here in this place connects back to the ghoul. Nothing can be solved until his dark energy is defeated. And this brings us to the final set of riddles.'

'There are more riddles? Why didn't you say so earlier?!' There was a note of frustration in Sophie's voice.

'Because, Sophie, earlier it was not the right time. Now it is, and you have asked what could be done. These things cannot happen until you are ready to ask for them. Now, this is what is known about the ghoul. It is knowledge collected by the brothers of the monastery.' The old man pulled a paper scroll from under his rags and unrolled it to read. Sophie felt a strange tinge of familiarity in his actions. Ralph coughed and cleared his throat before reading from the scroll. 'The ghoul cannot be defeated neither by metal nor rope nor poison nor stone nor fire nor water. Nor can he be defeated by someone who is either man or beast. He can only be defeated when it is neither day nor night; by someone who offers him a gift which is not a gift; and by someone who is neither eating nor fasting at the time.'

Sophie and Ralph looked at each other without blinking. Finally, Sophie said, 'let me work on that,' and lay down upon her blanket.

The darkness crept in around the small candle flames, and Sophie's mind dreamt of riddles.

CHAPTER EIGHT – GHOUL TOWER

*It's a certified fact, in any place you go, whether upside or downside,
that thoughts have their own life*

A hazy, light mist signaled the arrival of dawn. When Sophie stepped
out into the daylight she saw the landscape clearly for the first time. It
was as if she had arrived upon some desolate planet, strewn with ruins
and rubble, and a light red dust covered the land. There was no
vegetation, or greenery, or any other living creature. Then she noticed
the silence, or rather she *felt* the silence. It hit her like an empty-hearted
void. For Sophie, it felt like they were in an enclosed transparent
bubble, or dome, and the living world was shut out.

The ruins of the monastery, which Sophie had first thought was a large
mansion, were much larger than she had previously thought. The huge
ruined building stood alone upon a raised plateau that overlooked a
rock-strewn red desert that stretched as far as the horizon. Sophie
looked around in all directions – the view was the same except for one
thing. Behind the ruined monastery, in the distance, stood the tall
pointed green tower, shimmering like some luminescent mucus-

beacon. Sophie shuddered. The same strange energy from the night before filled the air, a gooey vibration that was as irritating as a bad smell. If she could wash it off she would, yet it seemed to stick to her invisibly.

Ralph came shuffling up to stand beside Sophie. 'Mm, this isn't the place it used to be. A fine land, and a lovely energy, all turned bad by this invasive stink.' He looked sadly into Sophie's eyes. 'This is what can happen when nasty thought-forms go on the rampage.'

'But they're just thoughts, Ralph. They're not weapons, or anything like that.'

Ralph shook his head and tutted. 'Sticks and stones may break bones, which heal, yet thoughts last forever.'

'Yes, but they're only in our heads. Thoughts don't actually leave our heads. They're private, and stay inside, which is probably a good thing. I wouldn't want some of my friends knowing my thoughts.'

'Thoughts don't leave your heads?! And where did you get that ridiculous notion from?'

'Well, *everybody* knows!' said Sophie, getting slightly exasperated.

Ralph rolled his eyes in his old scarred face. 'Well, I guess not *everybody* because that doesn't include me, or those of us in the Imaginal World.

I don't know who *your* everybody is, but they've certainly got the wrong end of the stick on this one. It's a certified fact, in any place you go, whether upside or downside, that thoughts have their own life. They don't just stay in pretty little heads. They leave and create thought-forms, which are then picked-up elsewhere. Does a television broadcast stay in the box? No, it leaves and travels – it *broadcasts* - and gets picked-up by thousands or millions of televisions everywhere. When you watch a TV program do the ideas just stay in the TV? No, they enter your own head and inspire you and make you think. It all moves around, connected, and everything relates to another thing. I'm sorry, but nothing stays private in your own little head. If thoughts stayed in people's heads, how would anything get created? How would painters paint and writers write, and designers design?'

'But we apply our thoughts.'

'Your thoughts? Whoever said they were *your* thoughts? Maybe you are a television rather than an antenna.'

Sophie looked puzzled.

'Maybe,' continued Ralph, 'you receive the thoughts - the broadcast - rather than creating them yourself. Thoughts come to you, and you just pick them up and you take them as your own. Have you ever *thought* of that?!' Ralph let out a low wheeze.

Sophie had to admit to herself that Ralph seemed to have a point, somewhere in all of this. 'And so this then, here - it's all because of a bad thought?'

'Well,' answered Ralph with a sigh, 'it's because of many bad thoughts. What happened here was worse than usual. It comes from a collective of angry thoughts, all shouting out at once in so many individual heads from your Regular World. You see, everybody has a little ghoul inside of them; a little nuisance thought. But if these little ghouls all get unleashed together, then what you end up with is something like you saw last night. And the energy they bring with them just flips the whole place over. Mm, something bad must have happened recently in the Regular World for this to happen here. Some kind of world-changing millennial event, I reckon.'

'Well, there was the...'

'Okay, what's your plan?' interrupted Ralph.

Sophie was briefly snapped out of her thoughts. 'Oh, err, we have to get to the tower. And it must be before the end of the day. I've been thinking about the riddles...' Sophie smiled, knowing how maybe, just maybe, the thoughts had not been her own.

'You have?' Ralph cocked an eye toward Sophie.

'Yes. And I've made a decision to do this. I know it needs to be done. I *feel* it.'

'Good. Then we make a move quick sharpish.'

'You still have that odd little yellow bird with you?' asked Sophie

'Always.' Ralph put his hand into a pocket of his ragged robe and brought out the yellow-feathered bird with longish red legs.

The journey through the red-dust wasteland was neither scenic nor eventful. And Sophie had to walk slower for Ralph to be able to hobble along with her. Ever since Sophie had answered correctly the ghoul's riddles and released Ralph from his confinement in the ruins, he had insisted on enjoying his new found freedom. Sophie had not been able to dissuade the old man from accompanying her upon the journey. On the contrary, he had insisted that he come along, and would not accept otherwise. Frail as he was, the old man seemed to have an untapped reserve of energy that surprised Sophie. Although slower than she was, he never once asked to stop or needed to rest. He shuffled along beside her, pointing out the places that once were, yet no longer remained. His memory appeared to be fully intact. In fact, the only thing damaged was his scarred face, like the landscape itself.

The haze of the sunlight bouncing off the red-dust created a strange orange-red glow that hovered over the land making it all eerily unreal. For Sophie, she imagined this was probably how Mars looked like, if anyone ever got to really walk on it instead of sending machines that broke down.

As they walked over the parched land Ralph continued to tell Sophie stories from his days as Abbott of the Monastery. He certainly seemed a chatty fellow, Sophie thought.

'So what exactly was the name of your monastery, anyway?'

Ralph's face lit up with a beam. 'Ah, now that's a good question. That's a question worth answering,' he said with a huge smile. 'Our monastery was called "The Monastery of the Sacred Blue Rose".'

'Blue rose? But roses aren't blue. They're red, yellow, white, pink, and, er, that's it I think. But I've never seen or heard of a blue rose.' Sophie gave one of her infrequent pouts.

'Oh, merciful me! Just because *you* have neither seen nor heard of a blue rose doesn't mean that it doesn't exist. Have you seen this thing called gravity? Have you seen love? Have you even seen your own face directly with your own eyes?'

Sophie stammered for an answer. 'Wait…now, love you don't see because it just *is*, and our face is in a place where we can't see it directly with our own eyes.'

Ralph snapped his fingers. 'Aha, and there you have it. Answered truly, even if you didn't realize it yourself! Things just often *are*, even when they exist outside of your limited senses. And the sacred Blue Rose is all about that, and so, so much more.' Ralph gave Sophie a wink.

Sophie knew that her plan depended upon reaching the luminescent monstrosity of a tower before darkness came, otherwise she would miss her opportunity. There was little time for rest throughout the day as the odd pair - an eleven year old girl and a scarred, large old man – went scrambling over ruins and dust dunes. Luckily, for the both of them, there were no mountains, canyons, or insurmountable obstacles to block their progress. On the contrary, the going was flat and tedious. Despite his ongoing yapping, Sophie actually welcomed the old man's company and his long tales.

'We had a popular story that was told often in the monastery. It was about a sinner and a worthy man with the stones. Do you want to hear it?'

Sophie shrugged. 'Sure - if we can keep walking.'

'Well,' continued Ralph after clearing his throat, 'the story takes place in the Regular World, of course, and is about a man who has lots of bad habits. For one, he's a gambler, and he loses more money than he wins. He's always upsetting people with the comments that he makes, even though he didn't mean to. He's the type of person who speaks before they think. He's also lazy, and since he lives alone his house is always a mess. He doesn't believe in the goodness of the world, and thinks that everything is just chance, and mostly bad luck at that. The result is that he resents and envies the world. Yet in his heart he is not a bad man. He is just weak, and he knows this - and this makes him even more miserable. So finally he thinks that he is a sinner, and that's that. Now one day a devout man, one who considers himself to be a good and worthy person, he decides he will help this sinner to change his ways. This worthy man decides that he will sit outside the house of the sinner, and every time he passes by the devout man will place a stone on a pile. That way, he thinks to himself, the sinner will see the pile of stones getting bigger and bigger, and the sight of this will make him feel guilty enough to change his ways. And so it came to pass that the man who considered himself worthy sat day after day outside the home of the sinner. And each time the sinner passed him by, another stone was placed on the pile. Soon the pile became two piles, then three, then four. In all this time the worthy man thought to himself that he was doing a service for the other man, and each time he put a stone on the pile he actually felt good about himself. In fact, it made him feel even more worthy. The sinner, on the other hand, only felt even worse. Every time he saw the pile of stones getting bigger and bigger it only made him feel less worthy, which caused him more misery. Instead of changing his ways, it only made the sinner feel worse about not being able to change. He actually thought that the worthy man was indeed such a good person, and far too worthy to be outside of his house. Each day the sinner would say a prayer for the worthy man that he may be blessed for trying to help him. And each day, the man outside the house would consider himself more worthy with each stone he put on the pile. Then one day there was a terrible earthquake that destroyed the whole house, and both men died at the same time. When they arrived at the Portal of Transition they were stopped by the Guardian of the Portal who checked their life-gained credentials. The Guardian immediately let the sinner pass through the portal, yet stopped the man who considered himself worthy. "You," said the Guardian, "must return from where you came until you have learned your lesson." The man, of course, protested his innocence and worthiness. The Guardian only replied – "what you did was only for yourself, and that was your choice. You gained your satisfaction from your actions. Yet the sinner had little choice, and when he did he prayed for you".'

Sophie waited until they had walked on a little further. 'And?'

'And what?' said Ralph with a shrug.

'So, what then?'

'Nothing – that's it!'

'Doesn't sound much like an ending to me,' protested Sophie.

'You've been watching too many films covered in sugar. You've stopped knowing how to think,' replied Ralph with a disconcerted grumble. Then he coughed again, and spluttered. Sophie was reminded of how fragile the old man was…or was it all just an act?

The hazy sun began to fall lower in the sky, signaling the coming of the day's end. Sophie knew she had little time in which to act. The riddles she had been given could only be solved under the right circumstances. They needed the right time, the right place, and the right people. Sophie sensed the riddles had been cleverly devised so that only a coming together of opportune circumstances could prevail.

SOPHIE'S SEARCH
FOR NO-WHERE

As they approached the ghoul tower they saw that it was glowing green because of some fungus or algae covering it, making it look prickly as well as ghastly.

'Look at that – looks like a moldy cucumber!' Sophie gasped at the height of the monstrosity.

Ralph lifted his head up high to view the tower's full length. 'More like an over-grown, over-worshipped gherkin. Maybe we should call it the *Ghoul's Gherkin.*' He chuckled. 'Whatever's in there, it has bad energy and it stinks.'

'Stinky or not, we have to get in and find the ghoul before we run out of time,' said Sophie looking at her wrist to check the time on her watch. For the first time she realized that she was not wearing a watch. Where had her favorite pink watch disappeared to? Oh well, she thought, I'm working with a different time now.

Before stepping through the large archway into the tower Sophie stopped and closed her eyes. She breathed deeply, and searched for a connection to herself; just as she had done when in Decision Hall. That time she had spent alone had taught her to find strength within her own self. She then bent down and picked up from the ground a tiny pebble, which she rubbed clean on her clothes and popped into her pocket. Then she stepped through the green glowing archway into the tower. Ralph hobbled behind cautiously.

If Sophie thought she was going to leave the luminescent green behind when inside the tower, then she was wrong. On the contrary, it glowed even stronger inside, as if the sun from the outside amplified the colors. This, thought Sophie, was what being in a real greenhouse was like…and it wasn't pleasant. There was also a smell of decay that lingered and clung like a damp atmosphere. Sophie wanted to spend as little time as possible in this place. The ground floor was empty save for a large stone table upon which stood some kind of sculpture. As she approached closer Sophie saw that it was a large clay mud figure of a boy, life-size and life-like, sitting on the table. So the ghoul enjoys making clay models of boys? Sophie thought that was very odd, yet she didn't have time to linger further. Across from the table was a doorway leading to a flight of stone stairs. Sophie turned to Ralph and asked him if he still had the yellow-feathered bird. Ralph nodded and brought out the bird from under his rags. Sophie reached out and without hesitation the odd looking bird jumped into her hand and chirped. She carefully folded her hand around the bird then, in no uncertain terms, told Ralph to stay where he was until she returned. Through a small glassless window of the tower Sophie could see that the sun was getting lower upon the horizon and would soon be setting.

She entered through the doorway and climbed the flight of stone stairs, feeling both anxious yet determined. She had made her choice, and this was the way it was going to be. And Sophie knew that when you make choices it's always best to stick with them, otherwise things start to get a little wishy-washy. After a few turns of the spiral stairs she entered upon a large room full of wall to wall mirrors. Stepping inside the room gave Sophie a feeling of disorientation. Everything she saw around her was distorted in the reflection of the mirrors. She stood still so as to maintain her balance. Sophie took a few seconds to calm and center herself. Then suddenly a loud gurgling noise arose and echoed all around her. Sophie shuddered, yet stepped forward into the middle of the room. All at once the image of the ghoul appeared in each of the mirrors simultaneously, and a deafening shriek shot out. Sophie breathed deep, remained still and regained her composure. Everything is in my head, she whispered to herself. I am in the Imaginal World – thought is power.

SOPHIE'S SEARCH
FOR NO-WHERE

'Hah, what is this? A little girl comes to my tower!'

The voice of the ghoul echoed out from each mirror and bounced around the room, creating a harrowing effect. Sophie's first reaction was to run; yet she stayed her ground, and tried the best she could to block out the mental invasion. She remembered what Ralph had said about receiving thoughts, and so she told herself she would not allow the ghoul's thoughts to enter into her mind.

'Little girlie, little girlie, lost in ghoulie's tower…!' came the taunting, self-satisfied voice of the ghoul.

'More like little ghoulie hiding behind mirrors is afraid of little girl,' called back Sophie.

'Afraid of nothing!' snapped the ghoul with a hiss.

'I have something for you. Why don't you meet me?'

'Meet, smeet, smithers, tithers, and tats!' jeered the ghoul from behind the mirrors.

'Your words cannot harm me. Now, come to meet me, or you shall forever be known as the ghoul who was afraid of a girl.' Sophie stood defiantly, and did her best to hide her nervousness.

'Choose the correct mirror and ye shall find me. Choose wrongly and thy shall fail… or do I mean fall?' The ghoul gargled once more and his image from all the mirrors disappeared.

SOPHIE'S SEARCH
FOR NO-WHERE

Sophie was left alone in the room of mirrors, with the sun setting and time fading fast. She had to choose a mirror, and there was no time to hesitate. But which one? Sophie closed her eyes and asked herself – which mirror would you choose Sophie? And then she visualized herself walking toward a mirror. She observed herself as if from outside, watching her own body move forward. She saw herself step toward a mirror directly to the right of her. That was it! She opened her eyes and looked toward the mirror to her right. Then she stepped toward it and reached out to touch its surface. Her hand disappeared into the mirror as if it were liquid. She knew what had to be done, without any further thinking – before her mind could protest. Sophie put her hand into her pocket and pulled out the small pebble she had collected earlier. She then placed the pebble in her mouth and stepped into and through the mirror.

'Not bad, little wanderer.' The ghoul snarled as Sophie stood in the foul-smelling room at the top of the tower. There were only a few feet between the two of them. From the high window she saw that the sun

had now dipped below the horizon and the last of its dying glow
shimmered in the air. It was now or never.

'Everyone has a secret, ghoul – and I know yours!'

The ghoul gurgled and spat on the floor. 'Don't think so, little girlie. I
rather think you're going to be my next prisoner.' The ghoul belched
and a foul smell left his filthy mouth.

Unperturbed, Sophie took another step forward. As any reasonable,
sensible person knows - you don't waste time when dealing with a
ghoul. 'I know that a ghoul cannot be defeated neither by metal nor
rope nor poison nor stone nor fire nor water. Nor can he be defeated
by someone who is either man or beast. He can only be defeated when
it is neither day nor night; by someone who is neither eating nor fasting
at the time; and by someone who offers him a gift which is not a gift.'
The ghoul hissed and spat again, yet said nothing.

'Well, I am neither man nor beast – I am a little girl, as you keep
reminding me. It is now neither day nor night, it is twilight. And I am
neither eating nor fasting, I am sucking on a pebble.' And saying that,
Sophie opened her mouth to show it was true. 'And now I am going to
offer you a gift which is not a gift.' Sophie held out her hand and
unfurled her fingers to reveal the strange yellow-plumed bird. The bird
flew toward the ghoul who tried to grab it.

'Yah, come 'ere, you're mine.' The ghoul jumped after the little bird as it darted away from him.

'It's your gift – but it's not yours!' called out Sophie as the bird flew toward the high tower window, with the ghoul leaping after it. And just as the ghoul made a last great leap to catch the bird, it swiftly nipped through the open window. Yet the ghoul was already in mid-jump and could not stop his momentum. He too slipped through the window. An almighty shriek could be heard as the ghoul went falling from the high tower to the bottom.

'Neither by metal nor rope nor poison nor stone nor fire nor water,' whispered Sophie quietly to herself. She then took the pebble from her mouth and threw it out the window after the ghoul. Abruptly a rumble and shudder shook the whole tower, and almost knocked Sophie off her feet. She turned and ran, leaving through the sole door of the tower room, whose stairs brought her once again into the room of mirrors. Without stopping for breath she ran down the spiral stone steps and emerged, panting for breath, in the first room of the tower. She looked about frantically for Ralph yet the old man was nowhere to be seen. The tower gave another huge shudder and shake, and finally began to collapse. There was nothing else to do but to get out quick.

SOPHIE'S SEARCH
FOR NO-WHERE

SOPHIE'S SEARCH
FOR NO-WHERE

Sophie ran out through the archway and back into the ruined land as a darkening sky crept overhead. Twilight was over. The night had arrived. Sophie kept running until she was exhausted. Only then did she look back to see the green luminescent tower crumble into dust.

Sophie lay back on the dusty ground, sweating and out of breath. Her eyes gazed up at the blood-red moon that was now in the night sky overhead. Yet something was not quite right with the moon. Sophie was sure she had seen it wobble. How could that be? Lying on her back, she fixed her gaze upon the blood-red moon. There was movement, she was sure of that. Then she realized what was happening. The moon was actually growing larger, like an expanding balloon. No, it wasn't that - the moon was coming closer and closer to where she was! It was moving faster and faster. It was now so large it almost filled the whole sky. Sophie's vision blurred blood-red and she covered her eyes with her hands and reached into the innermost depths of herself.

Whoosh! A huge burst shook the ground, and then she was drenched head to foot, soaking wet. Yet she kept her eyes closed, reaching inwards for her special connection…her lifeline to reality.

CHAPTER NINE – THE MONASTERY OF THE SACRED BLUE ROSE

You are never leaving when you are going forward toward your destiny. You will always be arriving

Sophie was drenched again as another wall of water hit her and completely soaked her. Yet still she clenched her hands tight over her eyes. Then she heard a deep, loud laugh.

'Come on, Sophie, open your eyes. What are you waiting for!?' Again, another deep laugh bellowed out.

Sophie opened her eyes and saw just in time as a handful of water was thrown over her.

'Hey, stop that! What do you think you're doing?' Out from under wet eyes Sophie saw a short, stout, bald man dance a little jiggle and then clap his hands.

'Sophie, she's awake and back from behind her cowering hands!'

Sophie pulled herself up from the floor and wiped the wet strands of her hair away from her face.

'I wasn't cowering behind anything. I was protecting myself from the falling moon.' As soon as she had said that the plump man bent over double in laughter.

'Hey, what's so funny?!' protested Sophie.

'Falling moon! That's a great one! I'll have to tell the boys back at the monastery about that one. Fantastic, love it – falling moon!'

Sophie looked at the plump fellow with the balding head, and noticed that he was wearing the robe of a monk. She looked at the man again, a little more closely. Although his face was chubby and ruddy, and was unfamiliar to her, there was something about the look in his eyes that Sophie recognized. She then took a long, slow look about her. She was standing by a fresh running stream within a meadow of blue flowers. Blue flowers? Sophie looked again and saw that they were all blue roses – and the place was full of them. Monk, monastery, blue roses…then it all suddenly clicked.

'Ah, the Monastery of the Sacred Blue Rose! So you're a monk at the monastery then?'

The portly man bowed with a smile. 'Not just any monk, Sophie – I'm the Head Abbott. Don't you recognize me?'

Sophie was stunned into silence. 'Noo, it can't be?!'

'Can be, is be,' replied the man with a chuckle.

'You can't be Ralph?'

'Can be, is be!' Again the man bowed and Sophie saw the shiny top of his balding head.

'But you were old and scarred before. Now…now, you look just like a monk should,' said Sophie with a gasp.

'Mm, yeah, a bit of a stereotype, I know. Yet I came first. The monks in the Regular World just copied my style. I've always been a bit of a trend setter in that way.' Ralph winked at Sophie.

'But how…?'

'Simple, really. It's all a question of vibration. When the ghoul came tumbling down, and everything else with him, then his dark energy left this place. Everything returned to its former lighter vibration. When things vibrate differently, you get a different configuration of how things come together. So, hey presto! There you have it - we're all back to how it was, and how it should be. Fine work by the way, dealing with that stinking cretin and his slime gherkin.'

Sophie was still trying to take it all in when a young boy, similar to her own age, came walking up. They looked at each other, in a few moments of utter stillness. It was the first time Sophie had met another person like herself in the Imaginal World. Until now it had been only herself and the odd inhabitants of this strange realm. Yet now, in front of her, was someone like herself.

The boy stepped forward. 'Hi, I'm Michael. Thanks for what you did back there. I thought I was gonna be stuck forever.'

The young boy was of similar height to Sophie and had shortish chestnut brown hair, parted to one side. He appeared to be a little timid. Sophie smiled and was about to introduce herself.

'Not at all!' burst in Ralph unexpectedly. 'If I hadn't of grabbed your good mud-self, squatting as a sculpture on that table on my way out, then you'd of been flattened and vaporized with the tower. But say nothing of it - a mere day's work for a monk.'

The three of them began walking through the meadow in the direction of the monastery, following Ralph's directions. Sophie and Michael chatted about their own adventures and how they had both arrived at where they were now. Michael told of how he had also followed the Green Man into the Imaginal World on a quest to find No-Where. Then he had met a strange old man in rags and white running shoes who picked him up in a solar-powered buggy before dropping him off

in some unknown place. He had then wandered into the darklands,
only to be caught by the ghoul when he couldn't answer his riddles.

Sophie laughed. 'Was the old guy in rags called Gabby by any chance?'

'Yeah, he was. And he was really grumpy too!'

Sophie nodded knowingly, and then tried as best she could to fill-in the details about her own travels. She mentioned about her own meeting with Gabby, but omitting the bit about vanishing into a column of flame and light. After all, who would believe that? Sophie also spoke of how Gali's house had been burnt down and then her meeting with the old lady Ketav, and her darling Starling. After that how she had entered the Forest of Fernacles and almost had it when Borik the Harkone got her all tied up. She didn't know what might have happened if it wasn't for the lovely Huffalots coming along to save her. Then she described how she had escaped on the boat with the greatest sea captain she had ever met - Jimbob the Oldest Sproggit. And then, after the vortex, how they had landed on Snifflegruff Island. And things didn't go so well with the charming-yet-very odd Snifflegruffs. Well, after all that – and after choosing a door for her own exile – how she too had ended up in the darklands. And that was about that.

'Phew,' said Michael with a whistle after he had heard Sophie's entire story. 'That makes my adventure with the grouchy Gabby sound like a run in the park.'

Sophie was a little curious about how Gabby had managed to meet the both of them, and no doubt at similar times…yet she decided to dismiss the thought. She had come to realize that in the Imaginal World the rational mind doesn't stand much of a chance. Then Sophie thought about her own adventures. Wasn't she missing someone? At that point there was a whoosh of air and a colored blur ran past her eyes. Ralph, Michael, and Sophie all stopped in their tracks as what appeared to be a large yellow-feathered creature with long dangly red legs went running, hopping, and leaping in a circle around them.

'Hey-ho, ho-de-hey! Eddie the Gangly here, don't forget about me. There's no threesome without a fine-feathered foursome!'

Sophie shook her head. 'Of course, Eddie the Gangly bird, that's who I was missing,' she said with a laugh.

Eddie came hopping to a halt and high-fived the air.

'Wow, hey, woo, wasn't that a ride back there. Small as a twitter-roo I was. Poor Ralph here had to carry me in his rotten pocket. And didn't that stink like putrid potatoes! I really don't dig it when vibrations go all low and dense on me. It just isn't cool – it's not Imaginal, that's what it's not. You Regulars really need to watch your vibration emissions or you'll mess us all up. What's happening in your world – lost the faith, brother?'

Sophie and Michael shrugged.

'Maybe the adults are just having a bad time,' suggested Michael.

'Bad time?' Eddie flapped his large yellow wings. 'I'd hate for them to have a worst time!'

'That's why we need to get to No-Place, and find No-Where as soon as we can. I know it's something to do with that, and it's all connected,' added Sophie.

'It sure is - surer than a plate of sureness. Everything's connected and there's no wiggle room out of that. Talking of wiggling, you did cool good back there in the tower, Sophie. Your answers were vibratory spot on! You've got the connection, I mean the real connection, and I can sense that. Hey, Ralph my man, what you say about that?'

'She's onto it alright,' agreed Ralph.

'And did you see the way I flew right past that green-brained ghoul and straight out the window? And how that oaf then fell right out the window after me…a Gangly bird masterstroke.'

'Sure thing, Eddie,' agreed Ralph.

Sophie stopped walking and looked Eddie straight in the eye. 'The last time I saw you was when you dropped me off at the Forest of Fernacles. How did you get all the way here?'

'All the way? What *all the way* do you mean? The Forest of Fernacles is just nearby – it's over there.' Eddie flapped his large yellow-feathered wing as if pointing away from where they were standing.

Sophie frowned. 'It's not just over there, Eddie. I had to travel a long, long way by boat first to even begin to arrive here.'

Eddie shook his large beaked head. 'Noo, you came by the route less traveled. The Forest of Fernacles is just next door if you travel as a bird walks. But you, well I think you went sideways and then down a bit. Talk about taking the long way to arrive here!' Eddie smiled and placed one of his wings on Sophie's shoulder as if to comfort her.

Sophie laughed. 'Typical. Just like me to never take the easy route.'

'I don't think traveling in a solar-powered buggy with a crazy irritable old man called Gabby is exactly an easy route either!' joked Michael.

Ralph smiled broadly and clapped his hands together. 'Exactly. You both drive the point home with excellent clarity.'

Sophie and Michael both looked at Ralph and then at each other.

'I mean,' continued Ralph, 'that the way you are seeking can never be a straight route. Straight routes don't exist for where you need to go.

You cannot arrive at your destination unprepared by your journey – it just wouldn't work. And you can only truly arrive where you're heading if, and when, the journey decides you are ready to arrive. Otherwise you'll just be forced to continue on your journey. Both journey and destination work together. They're both in cahoots with each other.'

Ralph laughed and skipped along as if pleased with himself. Sophie, Michael, and Eddie followed behind.

The four of them, walking together like old friends, arrived at the Monastery of the Sacred Blue Rose. Only that this time it wasn't a ruin but a magnificent cathedral surrounded by various other old stone buildings. Ralph had a beaming grin on his face as he marched in.

'Guys, I'm home!'

Sophie, Michael, and Eddie couldn't stop themselves from smiling at Ralph's boyish antics. Soon the entrance hall of the monastery began to fill with fellow monks – all Ralph's brothers – who greeted him warmly as if he had just returned from a normal excursion. Nothing, it seemed, surprised people in the Imaginal World. All possibilities were accepted and all potentialities allowed for.

Sophie and Michael went out together to stroll around the buildings and to gaze at their magnificence. The monastery was almost like a small self-contained village, with the monks also working in the fields growing their own food. There were workshops to make and mend objects, rooms to study and learn, kitchens to prepare and cook, and places for silent retreat. As they strolled around exploring the monastery buildings Michael shared his story with Sophie. He was an only child, a young boy growing up with his father after the early death of his mother. Life had been hard for Michael, and his imagination had always been a way for him to cope with his difficult life circumstances. Michael liked to draw pictures, and to create his own adventures where rules were different and where people didn't think out-of-the-box but without any boxes at all. In Michael's world, boxes were for people who couldn't think for themselves. He didn't want to see another square thought again – every thought had to be a new shape, brilliantly new. That's what he told Sophie, who listened patiently. Then Sophie told Michael about what the 'old Ralph' had said about thoughts not being owned by people, but that people received thoughts rather than produced them.

'That sounds about right to me,' Michael had said afterwards. 'I don't want to own my thoughts anyway. I'd much rather share them.'

Sophie both agreed and empathized with Michael. He was so unlike the other kids she knew from school and from her classes. He was more sensitive than all the other boys she knew. That was probably why he had gained access to the Imaginal World, thought Sophie.

Later that day Ralph invited Sophie and Michael to have dinner together with the brethren of the monastery, whilst Eddie went out to pick flowers before the sun set. Everyone ate together in the Great Hall amid great joy and laughter. All the monks of the monastery were extra kind to Sophie and Michael, and each tried their best to out-joke the other. If the monk's jokes were a piece of thread, it would stretch more than half-way around the world, joked Sophie to Michael.

'I thought monks had to take a vow of silence?'

Ralph looked over at Michael who had just asked the question. His face was complete seriousness, until he broke out into a fit of giggles. Ralph then banged the table with his fist as he roared in laughter.

'Monks in silence, you say?! Haha, that'll never happen! Never in a month of moondays! D'you hear that guys – this little fellow here thinks that monks take a vow of silence!'

The dining hall erupted into fits of laughter. It was quite a sight seeing such a jovial bunch of monks, slapping themselves on the backs, clapping, and breaking out into song. Even Sophie and Michael got caught up with the giggles and found themselves laughing along with the jolly monks of the Monastery of the Sacred Blue Rose.

'I'm not sure if I'd like to meet any monks from the Regular World,' said Ralph after he had finally recovered from the giggles. 'I bet they're a right bunch of stiffs. Are they like this?' And Ralph pulled a very long, solemn face; which was a little difficult considering he had a face as round as a pumpkin.

'Sure are!' said Michael. 'They're all so serious. People looking for peace are often so dull and serious. Sometimes it doesn't make sense to me.'

'Well, little chappie, sometimes if you wish to make sense of things then first you must lose your sense!' Ralph licked his lips, evidently enjoying his food. 'The Regular World often gets it so wrong, so lopsided and up-down and back-to-front. Here in the Imaginal World nothing is broken and nothing is wrong, it's just different. There is a different perception of things here, and its peoples' perceptions that have to change first.'

Ralph was about to say something else yet he decided to scrape up another spoonful of food instead. Evidently his hunger had made him change his mind.

'So, what is it you actually *do* here?' asked Sophie after she had let Ralph eat in peace for several minutes.

'Do?'

'Yes, I mean - do you just pray?'

'*Just* pray? We don't do *any* praying – we're a sacred monastery, my girl! What we do here is much more important. We write stories. We write the *word*. Without stories, jokes, riddles, and all the rest, how would knowledge ever get transmitted? Stories have the power to last forever, once they've entered the continuous thought-streams that circulate. Yes, this is a *very* special monastery.' Ralph chased what looked like a purple potato around his plate until he eventually caught it.

After dinner Ralph suggested that the three of them talk alone, away from all "my brothers" as he called them. There were other matters to discuss that required greater privacy. So they met in the Head Abbott's quarters later that evening. Ralph, Sophie, and Michael stood on a high terrace of the monastery observing the starry night above them.

It was Ralph who broke the silence first, which was not unexpected since he seemed to have a natural proclivity for speaking.

'Ah, it is truly beautiful here in this world. The Imaginal World would not be what it is without our continual connection to it. Do you know what people in the Regular World suffer from most, and which is the cause of most of their dis-ease? It's their "disconnection" – they've disconnected themselves from almost everything. They stopped themselves from reaching up to touch the stars.' And saying that, Ralph reached out and, in what seemed impossible, spun a star around in the night sky. Amazed, Sophie and Michael stood gazing as the star continued spinning in the firmament above.

'The Regular World lives with massive amounts of dis-ease,' continued Ralph, 'because it doesn't know how to let go of out-worn and out-grown ideas. It only makes it harder for the Imaginal World to pump out new imaginative ideas back into the Regular World.'

'And how exactly is that done?' asked Sophie.

'Well, this is perhaps why you are here. I sense it has something to do with your quest. It all works through dreams, you see. Somehow, we know that here in the Imaginal World we are able to seed ideas and patterns into the Regular World through people's dreams. And when people come across these patterns, and respond to them, they are unknowingly connecting to the source here. Again, it's all to do with connection, my dear. You've felt the connection, haven't you?'

Sophie nodded, then turned to Michael and saw the confused look on his face. 'It's true,' she said. 'It's all about connection – and we have to start with ourselves. There's something inside of us that belongs here, in this world. I can feel it. I'm sure it will help us be guided somehow, or at least to be connected to this place. Michael, you have to look for it too. Maybe this will help us find No-Where. I have a feeling that this No-Place and No-Where is connected with us – with something inside of us!'

Michael nodded. He didn't say anything at first, yet the expression on his face said that he understood. Then he turned to Ralph. 'Ralph, you must know something about this No-Place. Can you help us get there, and to find No-Where?'

The three of them stood around a large stone table inside the Head Abbott's office.

'This would make a great table for table football,' commented Michael.

'Ah, the tribal tendencies!' muttered Ralph under his breath, with a side wink at Sophie. Ralph went to one of his old wooden shelves and pulled down a large rolled-up scroll. Unraveling it he spread it across the table for Sophie and Michael to see. It was some sort of large map, with many wiggly lines and strange characters on it.

'I don't think it makes much sense to me,' said Sophie.

'Nor to me,' agreed Michael.

'Me neither,' added Ralph.

Sophie and Michael looked at Ralph, speechless.

'Hey, only kidding! I'm not called Head Abbott for nothing, you know. We hold great sacred secrets within these walls - and this sacred map is one of them.'

'So then, what exactly does it tell us?' Sophie peered over the map to get a closer look.

'It tells us where things are in relation to one another. And here in the Imaginal World it's all about relations. We don't do straight lines here, as you know. We work on the interconnections, where one thing leads to another.'

'And which thing can help lead us to No-Place then?' asked Michael, now also leaning forward.

'And help us find No-Where,' added Sophie.

'Good question - and the correct question!' replied Ralph nodding. 'If there's one thing I know about No-Where it's that it doesn't let itself be known directly - if that makes any sense?' No one said anything, so Ralph continued. 'What I mean is that you can't get to No-Where directly from here. It's just impossible. And besides, that's not how things work here.'

'Yes, I know, it's all about interrelations.' Sophie smiled at Ralph.

'Exactly,' said Ralph with a grin back. 'So to get connected to No-Place you first need to go to this place.' Ralph put his finger on a spot on the map.

'And this place is which place?' asked Michael. If he had thought about his question a little bit more he would have entered into a moment of confusion. Luckily for Michael he decided not to ponder more on what he had just said.

'This place is the Land of Potentials, as it happens to be. And in this place you need to find the Invisible One. He will be able to tell you how to get to No-Place in order to find No-Where. Or at least I think he will. Maybe Eddie the Gangly can help you get there.'

'And how are we supposed to find this so-called Invisible One if he's invisible?' Sophie shrugged and looked over at Michael, who seemed to be thinking pretty much the same thing.

'Ah, you have a point there - but only half a point. I'd suggest you find the Invisible One by the indirect effects he makes on the world. Just like your gravity I believe. You can't see it, yet you know it's there by the effect it has on the world. You see, everything truly is connected!'

Ralph rolled up the map and gave it to Sophie. 'Here, take this.'

'But I thought you said it was a sacred map?'

'Oh, not to worry, I have lots of 'em. This monastery is full to the brim with sacred stuff, mostly copies of copies of course.'

Smiling, Ralph left the table and plumped himself into a large chair that, despite his own roundness, was far too large even for him. 'Well, soon time for re-connection and re-charging the batteries, me thinks. I suggest you both also get a good night's sleep. You've still a lot of journeying to do yet.'

In the morning Sophie and Michael found Eddie the Gangly madly hopping around the monastery courtyard flapping his large yellow-feathered wings. As soon as he saw Sophie and Michael he came bounding over to them.

'Great to see you, guys and gals! Look what Eddie's brought you.' Out from under his feathers popped a hand holding a bunch of blue roses.

SOPHIE'S SEARCH
FOR NO-WHERE

Sophie had forgotten about Eddie's strange ability to manifest hands from the first time they had met. The surprise was not lost on Michael who almost jumped back in shock.

'What? You don't like Eddie's gift? Got the googly-ganglies all of a sudden?'

Sophie reached out and took the bunch of blue roses from Eddie.

'They're lovely Eddie - perfect for starting a new adventure.'

'Aha, a new adventure! Great. Where to this time?'

'We need to get to the Land of Potentials, to find the Invisible One and to ask him how to get to No-Place so we can find No-Where,' said Michael, now suitably recovered from the surprise.

Eddie's beak twitched. 'Mm, that's a shame.'

'Why?'

'The Land of Potentials is a place I can't get to, or show you how to get to either. Ganglies don't go there. You see, its way too unpredictable, always shifting according to potentials. Well, fancy that!'

'Then how are we going to get there?' Michael looked deep in thought, as if he had just been handed an impenetrable mathematical equation.

'I'm sure there's a way. There's always a way - isn't there Eddie?'

Sophie gave Eddie one of her endearing smiles.

SOPHIE'S SEARCH
FOR NO-WHERE

Eddie let out a squawk, or something that mildly resembled a squawk.

'Sure, right about that Sophie. I think I know the perfect someone to help you get there. Leave it to me – we Ganglies have lots of useful friends. I'll be back in a hop, before you can say geroahwhhyyywaahh.' Eddie leapt away in huge bounds and was soon gone from sight.

'Good. Looks like we have the beginning of a plan,' said Sophie.

'I like beginnings,' replied Michael, smiling over at her.

Sophie and Michael spent the rest of the day exploring the monastery buildings and mingling with the monks. The two of them were surprised at the harmony between the monks as they worked and went about their business. The brothers of the monastery joked and poked together, laughed and worked out issues with never a harsh word or a frown. And when Sophie asked one of the brothers about this, he just smiled and said it was all because of the sacred blue rose. He also added that the sacred blue rose really *was* sacred, and not a copy - copies of the rose only exist in the Regular World. Here, he had said, was the original rose - and that's why they all smiled. Sophie wasn't sure what to make of it, yet likewise had no reason to doubt the monk. It was as good an answer as any.

Ralph came over to join them as they were watching a group of monks working in the fields.

'They're planting the new crops.' Ralph stood beside Sophie and Michael, watching his brothers in joyful work.

'They seem very happy to be working,' said Michael.

'They're not working as much as living. If what you do is what you are, then there's no separation. You're just living.'

'Tell that to my parents!' replied Sophie with a groan.

'And my dad,' added Michael.

'Hey, guys, put your back into it - you look like a bunch of grannies wearing sacks!' shouted Ralph. Some of the monks turned and waved, or made some similar yet odd hand gestures. Ralph giggled. 'What do you call a group of monks?'

'A band of brothers?' Michael smiled at his own joke.

'A squadron?' said Sophie wryly.

Ralph shook his head. 'At least you're both using your imagination. It's actually referred to as a *Menace of Monks*. No kidding, it's true. Look it up on Wackopedia if you don't believe me. I guess your society just isn't ready yet for the monkish way. Maybe we should start praying for once, that might help.'

Ralph strolled off leaving Sophie and Michael to their thoughts.

'Sometimes,' said Michael, 'Ralph can be the sweetest nut case.'

'A full sultana,' added Sophie.

Eddie the Gangly was never one for subtle arrivals. He burst through the front door of the monastery flapping his large feathered wings and gangly-squawking, or whatever it's called that the Ganglies do.

'She's coming! She's coming!' Eddie hopped and leapt through the corridors and halls of the monastery until he found Sophie and Michael, who were by now sitting quietly in the Hall of Empathy.

'She's coming - gotta get ready!'

'Sssh, this is a sacred place of connection.' Sophie gave Eddie a frown.

'Uh, er, well, not to mind, you can connect another time. You've got to prepare yourself for *Her*!'

'Who exactly is "Her"?' asked Michael in a hushed voice.

'*Her*, of course! The one who's going to take you to the Land of Potentials - the Drakona. She's gorgeous...and ever so golden cool. Quick, quick, come, come - we have to meet Ralph and get ready. She'll be here soon.' Eddie leapt away, all feathers flapping.

SOPHIE'S SEARCH
FOR NO-WHERE

Before long all four of them were waiting in the outside yard of the monastery when she arrived. Everyone gasped as the enormous golden creature flew in and landed. She was indeed gorgeous, just as Eddie had said. A golden dragon that landed with such delicacy, grace, and gentleness that Sophie and Michael were both in awe. The creature turned her head to face them and bowed.

'I am the Lady Drakona. It is my pleasure to be of service.' A soft, soothing voice floated out of the creature's mouth, more like a song than speech.

'Oh, you're lovely! Sophie blushed as soon as she had said that.

The golden creature appeared to give a slight smile. 'Thank you, my dear. I am that I am.'

Michael too could feel a strong, radiant energy coming from the Lady Drakona. It was an energy that was powerful and yet comforting, not forceful. He stepped forward and bowed his head in respect.

'Thank you for coming - we appreciate you agreeing to help us. We've been trying to reach No-Where, yet it seems almost impossible.'

'No-Where is only unreachable for those who believe they can't reach it.' The words floated like a melody.

As soon as the Lady Drakona had said this then Sophie felt a sense of recognition within her. She was sure she had heard this phrase said before. Was that possible?

'First, you need to seek out the Invisible One. He will advise you on your way to find No-Where. I can take you to where I feel his presence. The rest is up to you. Come to me, if you please.'

The Lady Drakona lowered her spectacular golden body to the floor.

Ralph turned to both Sophie and Michael and gave them each a big hug. 'Here's where you leave, now. But remember, you are never leaving when you are going forward toward your destiny. You will always be arriving! May your arrival be blessed - I hereby give you the official *sacred* blessing of the Order of the Sacred Blue Rose.' Saying this, Ralph brought out two blue roses from his robe and pinned one each onto Sophie and Michael. 'The way ahead is as open as your heart - travel lightly.'

Eddie the Gangly also approached Sophie and Michael with a sequence of little hops. 'Be good you two, and try not to mess things up!' He then leaned in closer and in a whisper said, 'Be polite to the Lady

Drakona, I put in a really good word for you both.' He then winked and hopped back.

Sophie and Michael thanked them both and then climbed onto the back of the Lady Drakona's silken, golden dragon body. They nestled in-between the joint of the two wings, and waved as the Lady Drakona gracefully rose up into the sky. As they looked down they saw a *menace of monks* below all looking up and waving enthusiastically. Then they rose higher and higher until the fields of blue roses looked like a tranquil sea.

CHAPTER TEN – THE LAND OF POTENTIALS

*Everybody has a quest inside of them. It is whether you choose to follow it
that makes all the difference*

The mild air blew into their faces as Sophie and Michael dipped through the sky on the back of the Lady Drakona. They both felt completely safe riding with the huge golden creature, despite being so far above the ground that only colored blurs were visible below. For a short time all their concerns seemed to vanish, as if they had slipped into an altogether different time realm. Sophie felt an odd yet pleasant feeling within her, something like a warm buzz mixing the fantastical with the real. She also felt stronger within herself, as if she was more connected with things that existed both in and yet not in the world. Perhaps, she thought, it was an indication that she was getting closer to No-Place, and to finding No-Where. It was a feeling of being with the boundless, the expansive, where false limitations fade away. Sophie knew that the Regular World, where she lived and grew up, was filled with boundaries, fences, and frontiers. And not all of them could be justified. It was like they had just been put there as if a person were drawing their own map. Things were just so constrained in the Regular

World – so *artificial*. And yet here, flying high on the back of a great golden bird, everything felt more real. It felt real to Sophie because there was more possibilities…more freedom to fulfill one's own potential. She felt as if she was on a path unique to her, despite sharing it with others, such as Michael. And although she had been given the quest to find No-Where, it still felt like it was her very own journey. She looked across at Michael and she thought she saw something similar in his face also. Michael's face was lit up and alive with energy and that 'something extra' that Sophie didn't find in the faces of her class mates. Maybe, thought Sophie, this is the energy of potential that comes alive during the journey. Whatever was going to happen from now on, Sophie realized she was never going to be the same person, or be able to look at her world in the same way again. Sophie had arrived at a new place within herself, and all the worlds were now open.

All of a sudden the rush of air turned into a warm stream, as if they had just entered into a bubble. The Lady Drakona turned her head in mid-flight to check on her traveling guests. She spoke for the first time, above the rush of the warm air. 'We've just crossed into the Land of

Potentials. Soon I should begin to sense the presence of the Invisible One. I need to fly lower.'

The Lady Drakona then began to descend through the clouds, until finally the land below burst through with a spectacle of vibrant colors. Both Sophie and Michael were amazed at the display of vivacious flushes and tints that seemed to rise from the ground below. The Lady Drakona let out a soft laugh. 'Don't let your eyes deceive you. The Land of Potentials can be both vibrant and alive, as well as a prison of the mind. Everything has a potential here.'

Sophie and Michael held on tight in their snug position on the back of their golden host as she descended lower. The ground beneath them was like a painter's palette, with blues and yellows mixed with green and violets.

'It's like a rainbow world!' shouted Sophie into Michael's ear.

Michael nodded and smiled. 'A mixed bag of possibilities!'

With grace and care the Lady Drakona set her large winged body down within a field of black flowers. The golden beauty of the Lady Drakona looked stunning against the backdrop of the black flowers. Sophie and Michael carefully climbed down onto the land.

'Go on, you can pick a flower – they're safe,' said the Lady Drakona in a motherly way.

Sophie picked a flower and stared and it. Then she smelled it, and was surprised when it smelt of the sea.

'It's a Black Orchid. They are special flowers that carry the salt of the sea with them, yet they thrive on the land. They embody both water and earth. They bring both elements together into one, and that is why they are considered a flower of great harmony.' The Lady Drakona saw Sophie's confusion. 'Yes, I know – they are black. Black is often considered to be something negative. Yet black is also a color and energy of great elegance – and power. Black can be either the complete absorption of light, or its total absence. These Black Orchids absorb all the light they receive. You could say that they are flowers of complete light that shine iridescent inside.'

The Lady Drakona bent towards Sophie and blew upon the flower. As it came apart it released a flash of bright light.

'Cool,' said Michael as he picked a flower for himself and blew hard upon it. There was another flash of light as the petals separated from the stem and floated into the air. He was about to grab for another one as the Lady Drakona drew up close to the young children.

'The power to destroy is not as great as the power to create and nurture. It is only more tempting, that is all.'

Michael blushed and pulled his hand back.

Sophie looked into the sapphire blue deep eyes of the Lady Drakona. She sensed an immensity of energy and protection radiating from her.

'Where to now?' she asked.

The Lady Drakona raised her head and nodded to the distance. 'The Invisible One is near here. I sense his presence.'

'How do you sense his presence?' interrupted Michael.

The golden winged-creature let out a gentle snort that sounded like a sudden rush of air. 'His presence is by vibration. We all vibrate – some more than others. I feel presence by vibration more than I do by sight. We can be deceived by what we see. People deceive others by what they do, by what they show or say. Yet our vibrations only hold our true presence. A bad person cannot give good vibrations no matter how hard they try to deceive.'

'And what about us - can *we* sense through vibration?'

The Lady Drakona cocked her head as she looked at Michael. 'In a way, yes you can. Trust your instinct. Trust your deepest feelings. It is the heart that senses the vibrations, not the mind. This is the silent language that operates between us. It is older than speech, and existed long before the alphabet. It is the eternal language. You could say it is also the language of dreams.'

With the word "dreams" Sophie was jolted out of her reverie.

'Can this silent language help us to get to No-Place and to find No-Where?' she asked.

'Yes, of course. This is the internal thread that connects you. It is the silver cord that will guide you on your quest. Everybody has a quest inside of them. It is whether you choose to follow it that makes all the difference.'

The Lady Drakona stood back on her feet and stretched her body up to full height. She was such an incredibly large creature. Sophie was sure she could scare just about anyone if she so wished. Gracefully, the Lady Drakona brought herself down and crouched besides Sophie and Michael.

'It is not just physical strength that will help you through your life – it is also the strength to dream. The reality that you build with your mind can be just as real as any world outside of you. That's why we have to keep the power of imagination. Here in the Imaginal World is where we experiment with those creative potentials – call them dreams, wishful thinking, daydreaming, whatever – they all come here to the Imaginal World. It is said that there are those who dwell in No-Where that are responsible for observing and managing these imaginations. It is these imaginings which filter through to form the comings and goings of events for those of you in the Regular World. My dear children, never forget that in dreams begin responsibilities. Now off you go. Do not hesitate upon your next step. The Lady Drakona, and all the Drakonians, will keep you in our heart vibrations.'

The golden-winged creature that was the Lady Drakona flapped her wings and rose slowly into the air. With a flick of her head, which looked to Sophie and Michael like a salute, she sped away into the distance. Her figure became a golden color speckled against the rich blues, whites, and indigos of the sky.

Sophie and Michael stepped out of the field of Black Orchids and into a lane that ran past. They began walking in the direction as indicated by the Lady Drakona, uncertain of what to expect or to where they were heading. The colors of everything around them were bright and vibrant, as if glowing with their own sparkling energy. In fact, the colors were so bright that things began to look like they had just been drawn by an animator. If there was a hidden hand behind the whole scene then this wouldn't be surprising to any of us – including you and me.

Michael looked at Sophie and shrugged.

'You know what? I feel like we've just stepped into some kind of animation. Y'know, like this is a film or something.'

'I get the same feeling,' agreed Sophie.

They both looked at their arms, and then down at their legs. Then they looked hard at each other, and burst out laughing.

Michael pointed at Sophie as he bent double in laughter. 'You look like you're a cartoon Sophie!'

'And you a cartoon Michael - you look so weird!'

Then both of them began to jump up and down and thrash their arms around, as if they were indeed cartoon characters. They were so engrossed in their fun that they didn't notice the speeding car that came hurtling around the corner accompanied by the sound of huge stamping feet as the car braked suddenly, throwing up dust everywhere. Both Sophie and Michael abruptly halted, their hearts in shock, as they just realized they had barely missed being run over by a large black car with hairy feet…wait, hairy feet? When the dust finally settled they saw what looked to be a long, black limousine car with darkened windows and, yes, with hairy feet instead of wheels. The car gradually reversed, foot by foot, to where they were standing and the rear window slowly pulled down. It was so dark inside the car neither Sophie nor Michael could see anything at first. They came closer to the window.

'I'm sorry, we didn't see you. You came so fast,' apologized Sophie.

'So fast! Nonsense, you pickled pumpkin. I'll tell you what's fast – my patience, that's what's fast, you numbskull!'

'Hey, no need to be rude. I was only saying sorry.'

'Sorry is for younglings, for scardy-poos – for inkyblots!'

'What are you on about? I don't understand what you mean.' Sophie stepped back from the car window.

'Hey mister, we're sorry that's all. Everybody's okay, no harm done,' added Michael as he stood closer to Sophie.

A long, thin, wrinkled finger came out of the window of the darkened car and pointed directly at the both of them.

'No harm done!? What do you tourist-freaks know about *doing*, you pair of lemon tarts! You just made Blackheart Jake late…and NO-ONE makes Blackheart Jake late…for anything! If I ever see you pair again I'll turn your toenails into toothpicks. Now get out of my way, or I'll get in yours!'

The long, thin, wrinkled finger retracted back into the blackened depths of the car as the window pulled up. The black limousine pulled away with a feet spin and foot-screech as it roared onwards down the lane. Dust blew up in its aftermath and sprinkled the colorful day with a dirty mist.

'Wow, he was one rude dude,' said Michael as the car had gone out of sight.

'He was the pickled pumpkin, not us,' added Sophie.

'Sure was. It looked like he'd had his finger dipped in pickle too long as well.' Michael began laughing again, which eased the tension. Sophie was glad to have Michael's company; someone to share the road with, even if the journey is always one's own.

They continued walking down the lane, in the direction the limousine had taken. They began chatting about their lives in the Regular World, their classes and their school days. They found that they both shared remarkably similar experiences; although not in their regular lives, for Michael led a very different life from Sophie. Michael was an only child whose father could be considered to be quite well off. And being the only child of a rich parent he was spoilt from an early age with toys, games, and the latest gadgets. Yet the downside of being the only child of a rich parent was that he spent so very little time with his father. His closest companion was his nanny – a Philippine lady who lived with the family. She was kind and funny, and became a sole source of affection for Michael. In the absence of family affection Michael drifted more and more into his own world, and was a solitary young boy. Although he loved his gadgets, he soon came to realize that having all you want in the world is not enough. Then the real lack kicks in. Michael's quest began from his own sense of loneliness, and the feeling that there had to be more to the world beyond expensive gadgets and glitzy distractions. Sophie realized that the common link between them was a sense that the world they lived in was not all there was. And once you were able to see beyond this game of life…well, then things began to happen.

Their talk was suddenly interrupted by a thudding noise accompanied by grunts and huffing and puffing. When Sophie and Michael turned around they saw two figures running up behind them. The two men, dressed in uniform, came to a running halt beside them. One of the men was very tall and lean, and the other was small, rounded, and squat. Both men were sweating and out of breath, and had obviously been running for some time.

The small, squat man saluted. 'I'm Sergeant Spittlespat, and this is my colleague PC Wobblekirk.' The tall, thin man also saluted, and appeared to slightly wobble as he did so. 'We're on the lookout for Blackheart Jake. We know he came this way. Did you happen to see him?' As the sergeant spoke, little spittles of saliva jumped from his mouth.

'Erhh,' stammered Sophie, who was caught off-guard watching the man's saliva-lava.

'No erring, young lady. This is important police business. Blackheart Jake is the blackest heart in the entire realm. Hence the name, you see.'

'Hence the name,' repeated the taller man.

'Yes, thank you PC Wobblekirk. Well, he is wanted for a list of misdemeanors longer than all your arms put together, plus one…'

'Plus one,' repeated PC Wobblekirk.

'And maybe more that we are not aware of. That's always a possibility, of course.'

'Of course.'

'Yes, thank you, PC Wobblekirk. And well, you see, we need to speak with this fellow, Blackheart Jake, as soon as, or even before, possible. He's such a mean fellow. You know what I mean – he's kinda real mean like.'

'Real mean like.'

'Ahem. So, well, don't just stand there speechless. Speak up!'

'Speak up!'

'Have you, or did you – or have you not or did you not – see this Blackheart Jake pass this way?'

Sophie and Michael looked at each other, trying to keep straight faces.

'Does he have a big black car?' asked Michael.

'Yes!' replied both officers together.

'And long, thin, wrinkly fingers?' added Sophie, trying her best to hide a smile.

'Yes, yes!'

Sophie and Michael both stood there with blank expressions, taking time for a long pause. Finally, Sophie said 'Yes, I think we did. He went that way.'

'Phew, that's a relief,' muttered Sergeant Spittlespat, spitting as he spoke.

'A relief,' added PC Wobblekirk.

'Well, we best be off then. We have official business to deal with. And if you ever come across Blackheart Jake again, you both be mindful to keep right out of his way. He's as mean as a back-country fiddler with a broken string.' Sergeant Spittlespat seemed to add extra saliva-emphasis upon the final few words.

'With a broken string,' added PC Wobblekirk as he lent forward in a wobbly way.

Sophie and Michael nodded, trying to hide back their giggles. Then both officers saluted a final time and walked off at a brisk pace. Sergeant Spittlespat held a fast, stout walk whilst PC Wobblekirk, being as tall as he was lean, appeared to wobble from side to side as he kept up with the sergeant.

'What was that all about?' Michael shook his head in disbelief.

'No idea. But things just got a lot weirder very quickly,' replied Sophie.

'Maybe this Land of Potentials has just too much potential.'

'Meaning what?' asked Michael.

'Meaning that almost anything could be possible, and this may not be a good thing. Potentials may not always mean good ones. Its how they are used that matters - so we better watch out!'

The indigo-blue sky overhead appeared to buzz with intense color and a warm heat. Yet no sun could be seen despite the warmth. As they walked down the lane the two youngsters passed fields of bright reds, violets, oranges, greens, and yellows. It was as if they were immersed in some brighter-than-bright kaleidoscopic world. As they rounded a corner they saw up ahead what looked from the distance to be a walled town. The lane they were on led directly to the portcullis of the town and its possible only entrance. In the absence of any alternative, the both of them kept walking. It seemed a logical thing, albeit in an illogical place, to keep going down the path that was the only path. A diversion off the main path at this point would have been an illogical act in an illogical world which could, under logical circumstances, lead to some very irregular and unforeseen consequences. So Sophie and Michael thought it best to, well, to keep going forward on the only path available to them.

Soon Sophie and Michael were standing at the large wooden door which towered above them the full height of the wall. Michael was just about to knock when a voice buzzed in from out of nowhere.

'State your potential?'

'My potential?'

'State your potential to enter,' said the flat voice.

Michael looked at Sophie and shrugged. 'Er, my potential is that I have a great memory.'

'Memory potentials we already have. Entry not permitted.'

'What potentials do you need then?' asked Sophie.

'State your potential to enter,' repeated the monotone voice.

'I am a great runner!' said Michael in a burst of inspiration.

'Running potentials we already have. Entry not permitted.'

Michael's face showed frustration. He tried again. 'I know how to tell a good joke.'

'Humor potentials not in demand. Entry not permitted.'

SOPHIE'S SEARCH
FOR NO-WHERE

'Damn it. That's not fair!'

'Unfairness potentials we already have. Entry not permitted.'

'Oh shut up, you!' shouted Michael, feeling annoyed.

'Anger and annoyance potentials we already have. Entry not

permitted.'

Sophie pulled Michael away before he got himself more annoyed.

'Look, we have to trust ourselves on this. We all have potential, no

matter what it may be. Potentials are neither big nor small, they just *are*.

And maybe our potentials are not what the world expects of us.

Perhaps it's something special that we have inside – something that the

world doesn't, or cannot, see.'

Michael nodded and fell silent. Then a smile curled upon his lips. He

approached the door once again and said in a clear, confident voice. 'I

have the potential to know silence.'

'To know silence is a potential we do not have. Entry granted.'

The door disappeared and a shimmering curtain-like haze materialized.

Michael looked behind him to Sophie who just nodded and smiled.

Michael stepped forward into the shimmering haze and disappeared.

Immediately the solid wooden door reappeared again.

SOPHIE'S SEARCH
FOR NO-WHERE

Sophie stepped forward and cleared her throat.

'I have the potential to find the connection within me.'

'To find the connection within is a potential we do not have. Entry granted.'

The door once again disappeared and Sophie stepped forward and slipped through the shimmering portal.

CHAPTER ELEVEN – THE COLORLESS TOWN

You know who I am?

Something was not quite right. In fact, something was very distinctly different. It's like that feeling when you need to shake your head just in case something got stuck inside. As soon as Sophie stepped through the portal doorway she not only felt it immediately but she saw it too. Everything was in black and white - including herself! She looked at her arms and legs, hardly believing that she no longer had color. Sophie's first thought was that her eyes had been somehow affected by stepping through the portal. She hoped the effect would soon wear off. So, just to check, she did indeed shake her head – just in case something had gotten stuck inside. Then she felt slightly disoriented by the sudden change. It was a shock to shift from full animated color to a dull black and white world where everything seemed...well, seemed so grey. Michael came up to her and nodded without saying anything. Sophie saw that he too was feeling odd about the loss of color, and didn't know any more than Sophie about what was happening. Yet they didn't have time to say a word when a throng of cheers and noise filled the air. They had emerged into what looked like a large side street that ran parallel to the outer wall. The noise was coming from in front of them, down another street that ran perpendicular to the one they were on. They then noticed some figures moving up ahead.

'Come on, let's go,' said Sophie as she began to walk to where they had first seen the figures.

Michael followed her. 'Do we know what we're doing?'

'Not really. We're here to find the Invisible One, and we have to start somewhere. I just think that doing something right now is better than doing nothing.'

'Doing nothing can be useful sometimes,' protested Michael.

'I'm sure it can. But I just have a feeling that we need to move - to find out about this place. The more we know about this place the quicker it will be to find this so-called Invisible One. Remember what the Lady Drakona said about following our silver cord?'

Michael sensed she was right. Anything had to be better than standing still in a colorless world.

When they got to the end of the street they found that it led into a larger street where a throng of people were moving together in one direction. They joined this larger street, as did many others coming from smaller side streets. People of all ages and sizes - yet the same colorless bodies - were whispering excitedly amongst themselves.

'Michael, stay close. All these people seem a little odd.'

'You bet,' Michael replied. 'They all have the same silly basin haircut!'

'What?'

'Look - they all have the same haircut. It's what they called at school the basin haircut. Like the one some parents used to give their kids instead of taking them to the hairdressers. They would just stick a plastic basin on your head and cut around it.'

Sophie saw that Michael was right. Everyone had the same haircut, trimmed in a circle around their heads just above the eyes. It looked like everyone was wearing a neatly trimmed mop on their heads.

'Wow, you're right. Things just got even weirder. And listen, they're all whispering the same thing.'

Sophie and Michael listened to the whispering as it rose like a chant from the lips of the growing crowd - 'Ruu Eddin is going to speak...Ruu Eddin is going to speak.'

'Who do you think this Eddin person is?' asked Michael, somewhat bemused.

'That's what we're going to find out. Follow me.'

Sophie slipped through the crowds and tried to get further ahead. Michael followed closely, not wanting to lose her out of his sight. The throng of people, all moving slowly and almost in rhythm together, did not appear to notice Sophie and Michael pushing through. Or if they did, they didn't seem to mind, or care. Soon enough the street opened out onto a square, surrounded by high stone buildings that were equally as non-descriptive as the people. If this was the town square, thought Sophie, then the town itself had to be extremely dull – as well as being colorless. Not only was everything in monochrome, but even the appearance of everything in the town was of the most basic, and boring, design. The buildings were flat, expressionless blocks of stone with only a few small windows dotted here or there. The people that flocked around them all wore dark, non-distinctive clothes that hung shapeless off their bodies.

'If this is the so-called Land of Potentials, then the people here are way-lost!' whispered Michael into Sophie's ear. She nodded, knowing she had been thinking the very same thing. Talk about a contrast…

The expressionless crowd gathered around a small stage that had been set up at the far end of the square. Here, it seemed, everyone was waiting for someone to come - and speak. Sophie and Michael had

begun to feel some anticipation over what was about to happen. Yet

looking around them they saw nothing of the same in the people

gathered. Their flat, expressionless faces said nothing; only their lips

moved to whisper the chant that moved through the crowd like a

hypnotic drone - 'Ruu Eddin is going to speak…Ruu Eddin is going to

speak.'

'I wish he would hurry up and speak,' whispered Michael, 'or I might

fall asleep.'

Suddenly a hush came over the crowd as a figure with raised arms

stepped onto the stage.

Sophie's eyes widened. Now, she hadn't expected that. 'Wow - he's in

color! The first person in color we've seen here.'

Michael nodded in agreement, himself speechless.

The colorful figure lowered his arms and stood amidst the silence,

surveying the crowd. His eyes fell upon Sophie and Michael and

appeared to linger a second longer than normal. Not only was the

figure in color, but he was in the most colorful clothes possible. He

was wearing a long multi-colored robe that went from his shoulders to the floor. The man was tall, wiry, and thin looking, with a similarly long, thin reddish brown beard that added to his colorful appearance. He looked neither young nor old; so Sophie guessed he must be somewhere in the middle.

'You know who I am?' called out the man in a loud, clear voice.

'Yes!' replied the crowd in unison.

'I am the one who has stared at the sun.'

'Yes!'

'I am the one who changes from nothing to one!'

'Yes!'

'You cannot follow me.'

'Yes!'

'I cannot follow you.'

'Yes!'

'There is a distance between us.'

'Yes!'

'We all love banana cake!'

'Yes!'

'You know who I am?'

'Yes!'

'Who am I?'

'Ruu Eddin…Ruu Eddin…Ruu Eddin…'

'I think this Ruu Eddin guy is a bit of a banana cake himself.' Michael shook his head in disbelief and Sophie laughed into her hand. Then Ruu Eddin raised his hands once more until he had the crowd's full attention.

'Do you know what I am going to say to you today?'

'Yes!' replied the crowd in unison.

A big smile appeared across Ruu Eddin's face. 'In that case, there is no need for me to tell you. You already know! I'm going home. Goodbye.' Then the crazy thin man left the stage and walked away. The people in the crowd all turned to look at each other and shrugged. Their empty faces remained as empty as they had been before. Then without another word, or whisper, they began to disperse. Sophie and Michael remained where they were, standing close to the stage. They were unsure what to do next. As the large crowd of people was dispersing the wiry and colorful man called Ruu Eddin returned to the stage.

'You know who I am?' he called out again.

'Yes!' replied the crowd as they had begun to return to the stage.

'Who am I?'

'Ruu Eddin…Ruu Eddin…Ruu Eddin…'

SOPHIE'S SEARCH
FOR NO-WHERE

'Do you know what I am going to say to you today?'

There was a silent pause amongst the crowd before they replied in unison, 'No!'

Again, a big smile appeared across the colorful man's face. 'In that case, you are not yet ready to hear my message. I shall come back when you are more prepared. I'm going home!' Then he abruptly left the stage.

Once more, the crowd began to disperse and move away from the square.

'How many times is this going to happen?' mumbled Michael under his breath.

'Yeah,' agreed Sophie, 'I think it could get repetitious. But I have a feeling about this character. Look, if he's the only person here in color, then doesn't it make sense that he's the one who's the most visible?'

'And?'

'And, by contrast, he may know how to find the one who is the least visible – the Invisible One!'

'You know who I am?'

Ruu Eddin had returned quietly to the stage and had called out his now familiar greeting another time. Again, the crowd began to return to the front of the stage.

'Yes!' they all called out together.

'Who am I?'

'Ruu Eddin…Ruu Eddin…Ruu Eddin…'

'Do you know what I am going to say to you today?'

There was another long silent pause. This time Sophie decided it was time to add something to the gathering. She shouted out, 'Well, some of us here do, and some of us don't.'

Ruu Eddin's gaze fell upon Sophie. He stared at her for what seemed to Sophie to be an uncomfortably long time. Then a huge smile erupted over his face.

'In that case,' he began, 'those here who do know what I'm going to say can share it with those who don't know - and so you don't need me. I'm going home!' And again, the multi-colored figure left the stage.

'Come on, we need to follow him,' said Sophie quickly. They both pushed through the dispersing crowd and followed the colorful Ruu Eddin. It wasn't difficult to spot the only object of color in an otherwise dull colorless environment. Nor did it seem like he was trying to get away. Ruu Eddin was walking with a brisk pace that at the same time appeared somewhat leisurely. Sophie noticed that he walked

quite fast for a person of his stature. Then he turned a corner and was

out of sight. At that point both Sophie and Michael began to run. They

crossed the narrow street lined with the same unremarkable buildings

and hurried around the corner, and…*Wham!* They ran head on into a

group of people.

Several bodies fell upon the floor, including Sophie and Michael.

Sophie rubbed her head, feeling a little dazed. Then, for the second

time, she shook her head again– just in case something had gotten

stuck inside. When she looked again she saw a pair of the meanest eyes

staring at her from a scrunched-up angry face. A long thin, wrinkled

finger came up and wagged itself in front of Sophie's face.

'I told you to keep out of my way, you sack of rotten codfish.'

A thin, short, mean-looking man all dressed in a smart black suit was

lifted to his feet by three stout gentlemen similarly dressed in dark

suits.

'Are you okay, boss?' asked one of the stout men.

The mean-looking man brushed his jet-black greasy hair back over his

forehead and stared angrily at Sophie. She saw that his hawk-like nose was expanding and contracting rapidly almost like an over-worked pump.

'Do you know *who* I am?' rasped the angry man.

Sophie sighed. Oh please, not again, she thought. Doesn't anybody in this town know who they are?

'People know me as Blackheart Jake,' said the man, almost hissing. 'And you, you ungrateful sourpuss, have just made your last mistake. Grab her - and the boy too!' Two of the stout henchmen grabbed hold of Sophie and Michael. 'Let's see how you two like being pickled in a pickle! Blindfold and gag 'em, then bring 'em with us. They can be put with the other one.'

The colorless world suddenly got darker for Sophie and Michael, as they were first gagged, then blindfolded and lifted onto some hard, bony shoulders and carried off. At first they both struggled and let out muffled shouts, yet to no avail. Minutes could have been an hour. Time was no longer in synch with events. Everything for the both of them was just bumps, grunts, and jolts. So they had no choice but to endure the shaking and jerking darkness until the blindfolds were eventually taken off.

SOPHIE'S SEARCH
FOR NO-WHERE

The room was sparse, drab, and dim. From a low ceiling hung one dirty faintly lit light with no visible switch to turn it off. Even the grayness of the walls looked extra grey despite the general lack of color. There was no window or natural light; only a door with one small square viewing slot to peek through. Sophie was dumped onto a small cot with Michael left on another. There was another cot in the room which stood empty, yet it looked used with ruffled sheets and a tin plate by its side.

'This is a real dump. How did we get here?' If it was a question, it sounded like Michael was asking it to himself.

Sophie was sitting quiet and still on her cot, her eyes closed. Michael began to pace around the room, nervously. If it was one thing he especially didn't like it was being confined in small spaces. It wasn't that he was claustrophobic; it was more a sense of not being able to leave a place that worried him. In elevators it didn't affect him so much as he knew, more or less, that the door would open once he had reached his chosen floor. Yet after many experiences of being locked in his room by his busy, and often impatient, father he had learnt to dislike anything that restricted his freedom of movement.

'Don't let the outside distract you. Nothing is as it seems. You should know that by now. C'mon Michael, try to connect with your potential.' Sophie remained sitting quietly on her cot with eyes closed. Michael went and sat down and also entered into his silence – the place where he had potential.

'What's this, a pair of lemons looking lemony? It's so treacly and horribly sweet.' Blackheart Jake was peering through the slot and sneering. Then he became annoyed when he didn't receive an answer, or any reaction.

'Look 'ere you two lumbering carrots, Blackheart Jake has plans for you so you better pepper up and stop lounging like potatoes!'

Sophie opened one eye. 'Are you speaking to us?' she asked in a very calm and soft voice.

Blackheart Jake grunted. 'Of course I am! Do I look like someone who would be speaking to himself? Do I look like a half-baked vegetable?'

'I don't know. I'm not an expert on vegetables. But I do know you're the rudest man I've ever met.'

'You haven't met my brother, he's double blackhearted and ruder than a reddened radish with road-rage.'

'Well, I don't need to have met your brother to know that *you* are a real meanie.'

'Oi, now who's the one being rude?! Insult me again and I'll pickle you before you have time to say peppermint prunes.'

Sophie just sighed. 'What a bore you are, Blackheart Jake. When you're mean like that you're only being mean to yourself. It doesn't do you any good.'

Blackheart Jake snorted and slammed shut the door slot before storming off. Sophie breathed out in relief.

'You were taking a risk there speaking to him like that,' said Michael a little apprehensively.

Sophie shrugged. 'Maybe. But you know it's important not to play people's games. You have to take yourself out of *their* game and make a new one. Blackheart Jake wanted us to be afraid of him and to be scared, don't you see?'

Michael nodded in agreement. 'It's just not an easy thing to do. It's a normal reaction to be scared with people like him.'

'And that's exactly what he wants. But if you don't play along, if you make your own game-play, then it confuses them. They don't know what to do because they're not getting the reactions they expected. It throws them off, and that's a chance we need.'

'Where did you learn all that? Did you take a psychology class at school?'

'No, I'm only eleven Michael. We don't have psychology classes for eleven year olds. I don't know where I learnt it – maybe it was here in the Imaginal World. After all, everything here is about *how* we think and behave, and it affects everything else. Didn't you pick that up? How we behave here will affect how this world responds to us. That's why it's so important we find our own connection – it's all about *us* if we ever want to get to No-Place and find No-Where.'

Michael sat down and crossed his arms. 'Mm, I guess I'm still learning. I'm only ten, after all.'

The door rattled with keys and then squeaked loudly as it was opened. A stout, burly man dressed in a black suit entered and slid two tin plates across the floor to each cot.

'Eat – then work!' said the man in a gruff voice.

'Thank you,' replied Sophie smiling at him.

'Yes, thank you. Food looks real nice,' added Michael.

The man stopped and gave them both a funny look. He was about to say something else but then thought better of it. He left the room without another word and quietly closed the door behind him. The food on both plates looked like some kind of pulverized mush.

'I think, knowing Blackheart Jake, that it's going to be vegetables,' said Sophie with a wry smile.

'Black and white vegetable mash – now that's a first!' Michael laughed and began eating. The taste wasn't *that* bad…

All the while Sophie was considering how to make the best of this bad turn of events. She was sure that they were here for a reason; that it wasn't just bad luck. She couldn't figure out why in a town which was supposedly full of people with potentials there was seemingly such a lack? According to the portal where they had entered, the town was already full of potentials. What had gone wrong? The Lady Drakona had said that she sensed the presence of the Invisible One in this direction. Despite these seemingly separate parts, something had to fit together – she just *knew* it. Michael too was deep in his own thoughts, sitting silently with himself.

The metal door to their dingy room burst open.

'Oi, get up you two – its work time. You ain't 'ere for nothing.

Blackheart Jake says you got to earn your keep, or you don't be kept.'

Another stout nondescript man in a black suit stood before Sophie and

Michael.

'Okay, then don't keep us. We're happy to be let go for not earning our

keep,' replied Sophie with a smile.

The stout man frowned. 'You being funny with me?'

'No. I was just being logical,' pointed out Sophie.

'That ain't right – and I ain't buying it. Now move it!' The stout man

impatiently ushered the two of them out of the room. They walked

down a narrow corridor that was similarly dark and dingy with no

windows. They went down another two corridors exactly the same

until they arrived at another plain metal door. The stout man pushed

the door open and motioned for Sophie and Michael to enter.

It appeared as if they were in some sort of factory. The large room in

front of them was full of packing boxes, strangely shaped objects, and

in the centre was a large conveyor belt. It was another nondescript

room with two high windows on one wall. A short, thin fellow with a

pointed hawk nose and greased back hair marched over to where they

stood.

'Ah, the ungrateful workers are here. It's time for these inkyblots to be useful to Blackheart Jake. Make no mistake unless you want to end up pickled! Now, listen good. This is the children's department of my factory. Here we make the best toys to distract as many children as possible from their parents. And I make the best money. That's it – end of story. Now get cracking, you pair of lemon tarts!' Blackheart Jake marched away laughing to himself.

'Lucky children,' mumbled Sophie under her breath.

The stout man showed them what to do. There were four types of vegetable-themed rag dolls – Broccoli Babies, Cauliflower Kids, Pumpkin Punks, and Gherkin Goths. To Sophie and Michael they all looked equally hideous. Just odd shapes of rags badly stitched together with odd, scary faces stamped onto them. They were ordered to pack each variety of rag dolls into boxes and then place the boxes onto the conveyor belt for packing and stamping. It was monotonous work. After Sophie and Michael had demonstrated that they could do the work without supervision the stout henchman left the room with a grunt and locked the door.

'Maybe one of these ugly vegetable rag dolls is the Invisible One?' said Michael wryly.

'That would make the Invisible One very, very invisible,' replied Sophie as she looked into the grey face of a Broccoli Baby.

Sophie and Michael had little choice but to continue with the hideously tedious work of packing the ugly rag dolls into their boxes and placing them onto the conveyor belt. The drab factory room was oppressive and the both of them soon felt as if they were the rag dolls inside a box. And the thing about the human body is that once it does an action for long enough it becomes automated. The body is good in that way – it learns quickly and then takes over so the mind doesn't have to think much. That's how most of the work in the world gets done – by automated bodies.

Suddenly, something snapped Sophie and Michael out of their trance-like packing. A pleasant tune unexpectedly echoed around the factory room. Sophie and Michael looked at each other to make sure they weren't the only one hearing it. Then Michael saw him first. Through one of the high windows poked a cheery face, with a reddish brown beard that curled at the end.

'You whoo!? Who goes there?'

SOPHIE'S SEARCH
FOR NO-WHERE

Sophie and Michael stopped work and looked up at a smiling Ruu
Eddin.

'You know who I am?'

Sophie sighed. 'Yes, we know who you are.'

'You're Ruu Eddin,' added Michael.

The smile on Ruu Eddin's face disappeared. 'I'm going home –
goodbye!'

'Wait!' shouted Sophie. Yet the face was gone, and the window closed.

After what seemed like hours of packing endless boxes of ugly
vegetable rag dolls the stout man returned to take them back to their
dingy room. Yet this time when they entered their room they were met
with a surprise.

A girl with short dark hair looked up at them and smiled.

CHAPTER TWELVE – THE INVISIBLE ONE

There is no final end, there is only further

Arabella's dark round face lit up as soon as she saw Sophie and

Michael. She jumped up from the cot and could not stop from giving

each of them a huge hug. It was as if she had just found her lost

siblings. Arabella lost no time in recounting her own story of how she

came to find herself in the clutches of Blackheart Jake. She told how,

after following the Green Man into the Imaginal World, she managed

to get herself lost in the Curving Canyons. Luckily she met a small,

roundish man with balding hair and a jovial laugh who helped her.

'Ralph!' cried out Sophie and Michael together.

Then after traveling with Ralph and leaving the Curving Canyons they

came across a strange type of walking, talking bird that had hidden

hands.

'Eddie the Gangly!' laughed Sophie and Michael, who by now were

familiar with the story.

Arabella finally told how Eddie the Gangly had advised her to find the Invisible One and then helped her through a door in the air where she arrived at Snifflegruff Island.

Sophie threw up her hands.

'Yeah, I get it. You were looked after like a queen for a month and then thrown into exile?'

'You bet,' laughed Arabella. 'Those Snifflegruffs were the weirdest kind of nice I ever met – talk about mixed messages! Well, I then chose a door that brought me to the entrance of this place, the most boring town in the whole of the Imaginal World.'

Arabella giggled and shook her head. She was the type of girl that might be called 'mousey' – slightly darker skin, short dark hair and a pleasant, affable roundish face. Arabella told Sophie and Michael that she had just turned twelve years old and had been having those 'special dreams' for nearly a year before she was finally able to be lucid enough to find and grab hold of the Green Man. Unlike Sophie, Arabella had found the Green Man not in a garden but in a shopping centre.

'Wow!' exclaimed Michael. 'I thought it was strange that I always found him in an amusement park. It took me ages too before I could finally catch-up with him. Then we went through the door together.'

'Talking of doors,' said Sophie with a smile, 'what was your potential for getting into this town?'

Arabella sat back on her cot and rolled her eyes. 'My potential is also my Achilles heel sometimes – it is patience. And now my patience keeps me waiting here for a way out. Silly me, I guess. My father always told me I should be more pro-active. But I *always* made a point of not listening to my father's lectures.' Arabella winked and they all laughed.

'And Blackheart Jake?' asked Michael.

'That vegetable-obsessed ragamuffin bumped into me one day, then said it was my fault and that I'd bumped into him – then wallop! He bangs me up in here with his freak show. Oh yeah, another thing, don't mention anything about the "you-know-who" to him. I think it makes him angry. He's got this chip on his shoulder or something. That guy's real weird. Have you seen the way he slicks his hair back, like he's tough when he isn't?'

Sophie and Michael both laughed. They had taken an instant liking to this girl Arabella.

Michael leaned forward from his cot and asked in a whisper, 'The "you-know-who"?'

'Yes,' whispered back Arabella in a tone of conspiracy, 'the Invisible One.'

SOPHIE'S SEARCH
FOR NO-WHERE

The next morning a soggy sort of vegetable porridge was served for breakfast. Then the three of them were taken out of their room and marched to the factory. As before, Sophie and Michael were placed in the packing room with the large conveyor belt, and Arabella was taken elsewhere. Sophie and Michael soon learnt that Arabella had the job of putting the different faces onto the various vegetable rag dolls. Arabella later said that, 'You think you have the bad job. I have to deal with endless faceless vegetable babies. It's so freaky when they stare back at you for the first time.'

As they worked in the dingy factory room Sophie and Michael spoke in hushed tones together about how they could escape away from the place – and away from Blackheart Jake. First, they would need to get away from the hunky henchmen who followed them everywhere. Luckily for them, the henchmen were not the smartest trees in the forest. Yet the biggest problem was that they didn't know exactly where they were. They could not orientate themselves in the maze of dark, dingy corridors and endless identical metal doors.

'What if we escape from here only to find ourselves in another maze, one that's even worse?' said Michael in a hushed voice.

Sophie shook her head. 'We can't think like that. If we think in negatives then everything after will be a negative – and nothing good ever comes from negatives.'

They finally decided that the best way forward would be to collect as much information as possible from being attentive. Attention, said Sophie, was the key to understanding the situation, and that they had to remember everything. Sophie and Michael shared their thoughts with Arabella during their short lunch break, which consisted of vegetable puree with celery sticks.

'I'm never going to criticize rice again,' said Arabella with a hint of irony.

'Nor me, quinoa,' added Michael.

The other two looked at him.

'What? You've never had quinoa stuffed down your throats three times a week?' They all laughed. Then, as friends, they agreed to keep an eye open for each small detail during their time away from their shared room. Then they were shortly marched back to their respective factory rooms. And so another monotonous afternoon passed with the vegetable family of rag dolls.

Again, as they were working monotonously packing the boxes, Sophie and Michael heard a pleasant tune echo around them as if out of nowhere.

'You whoo!? Who goes there?'

The face of Ru Eddin once again poked through one of the high windows.

'You know who I am?'

This time Sophie hesitated before she answered. 'Maybe we do and maybe we don't,' she replied.

'Do *you* know who you are?' called out Michael.

A quizzical look appeared on Ruu Eddin's face. He then rolled his eyes upward as if he were thinking, although it was all a grand pretence. 'Maybe we does and maybe we don't. Goodbye.' And then he withdrew his head again and was gone.

Later that evening the three youngsters shared their thoughts and reflections upon the day. Sophie and Michael told how Ruu Eddin, for the second time, had poked his head through their window with the same nonsensical question as always. They recounted how they had heard him say the same things to the people gathered in the square. Arabella nodded thoughtfully as she listened to their story. 'Yes, I know,' she said finally, 'he comes to me everyday as well. And he asks the same question – do I know who he is? – and then he leaves again. I mean, really, what kind of help is that? It's about as helpful as a pair of roller-skates to a three-legged blind mouse!'

'Mm, nice analogy,' agreed Sophie, 'but there must be more to it.'

'Why would he come to all of us everyday? Who are we to him anyway?' added Michael.

'Maybe we're his amusement, just as we're Blackheart Jake's workers!' said Arabella disdainfully.

'No, it has to be more than that. I think it must be a clue or something. Nothing happens in the Imaginal World by accident. Everything is connected with everything else. That's what I've learnt here. We must find the connection.' Sophie sat back on her cot and went silent.

The next few days passed the same. It was a repetitive and tedious routine with the same meals, the same work, the same sights and the same black-suited henchmen marching them around. Every now and again Blackheart Jake himself would pop in to taunt the three youngsters. On one occasion Arabella decided to taunt him back.

'Hey there, inkyblots, how you all liking the luxury work here?' Blackheart Jake sneered at the three youngsters as he chewed on what looked like a carrot stick. Yet since everything was without color it could just have easily been a turnip stick.

'Oh, it's not too bad,' answered Arabella with a cool smile on her face.

'Bet you all wish you were someplace else, eh? Bet you all wish you hadn't of messed with Blackheart Jake, eh?' Blackheart Jake sniggered as he chewed.

'Well, we don't have to worry much longer,' replied Arabella with a feigned sigh, 'the Invisible One is coming to get us out soon. He said so himself.'

Blackheart Jake almost leapt in the air when he heard that. 'What!?' His carrot-turnip stick fell from his mouth and he began to splutter.

'You've been speaking with the Invisible One? He's been here? When?' Blackheart Jake looked as if he was about to foam at the mouth.

Well, he did communicate with us. But I can't exactly say if he was here or not – he's invisible, you see? Or rather, you don't see!' Arabella smiled and casually leaned back upon her cot.

Blackheart Jake couldn't tell if Arabella was telling the truth or just playing with him. He pointed his thin, wrinkly bony finger at all three of the youngsters. 'If any of you lemon tarts ever communicate with the Invisible One again, I'll pickle you all! And don't be playing with me either – Blackheart Jake doesn't play games or roll dice.' He then stamped his foot and left the room in a huff. His half-chewed vegetable stick remained on the floor where it had fallen.

'Nice one,' called out Michael when they were alone again.

Arabella just shrugged. 'I couldn't resist it. That pumped up nose picker is just too easy to poke.'

Sophie laughed, yet she was also lost in thought. Something Arabella had said had made her think, and a sudden realization had come to her.

The following day Sophie seemed quiet as if still lost in thought. The day passed the same as the previous days, and as the afternoon work shift began Sophie seemed apprehensive, regularly looking up at the high window. Soon enough, as on days past, an enchanting tune entered the factory room. Then a colorful head, with a reddish-brown pointy beard, popped through the high window.

'You whoo!? Who goes there?'

Sophie motioned to Michael to stay quiet. She wanted to take the lead on this one.

'You know who I am?'

This time Sophie didn't hesitate before she answered. 'Yes, we do. You are the one whom nobody sees. You are here and yet you are not. We know who you are – you are the Invisible One.'

A huge grin spread across the face of Ru Eddin, and then he stuck out his tongue before disappearing from the window. Sophie and Michael looked at each other, speechless. Had Sophie's gamble paid off?

A rope ladder suddenly dropped down from the window. Without wasting any more time Michael, then Sophie climbed up the ladder and through the open window above them. As soon as they had crawled out of the window they found themselves standing on solid ground. Their factory window had been at ground level, making their factory room, and all the other rooms, below ground. It made sense, after all; such dark and dingy rooms.

'And what about our friend, Arabella? We need to get her too.'

SOPHIE'S SEARCH
FOR NO-WHERE

Ruu Eddin hopped from one foot to the other and then skipped over to another low window and opened it. Sophie ran over and stuck her head through too. She saw Arabella below in an even smaller factory room, with a rag doll in her hands.

'Arabella, take the ladder and climb up. It's okay – we're leaving!'

Ruu Eddin dropped the ladder and they all helped Arabella through the window and onto solid ground.

'Follow me – the way ahead is visible!' Ruu Eddin waved for all three of them to follow him.

They ran through various backstreets and lanes, sometimes passing the passive populace who didn't seem quick enough to grasp what they were seeing. Eventually they arrived at an unremarkable door in a wall. On passing through the door they entered a wonderful, colored courtyard that lay beyond. It was filled with a beautiful array of flowers, including Black Orchids and Blue Roses. Colorful birds too were perched on alcoves above the stone courtyard. Then all three youngsters had the same realization together at the same time – they were in color! The rich colors they had experienced when they had first arrived in the Land of Potentials had come back to them. Everything seemed so amazingly bright.

SOPHIE'S SEARCH
FOR NO-WHERE

'I have to sit down,' said Michael. 'I feel so dizzy from seeing all these bright colors again.'

'I know what you mean,' agreed Arabella, 'it's kind of a shock. It's like when you think you see someone driving a car and then you realize it's not a person but a dog in a dinner jacket.'

Sophie too sat down, beside Arabella. 'I think we have to do something about your analogies,' she whispered.

Ruu Eddin prepared a most delicious feast that evening. Color and taste had finally come back into their food. The three youngsters ate with a renewed hunger and appetite, both for the colors and textures as well as the taste. They laughed and joked together, and Ruu Eddin told some wondrous and funny tales. Sophie noticed that throughout the evening both Michael and Arabella were throwing odd glances at her when they thought she wasn't looking.

Finally, as the evening turned quiet, Arabella spoke up. 'Okay then Sophie, you need to explain to us now. How did you know Ruu Eddin was the Invisible One? How did you get it?'

'Yeah, how did you figure that one out? It never occurred to me,' said Michael as he sat back sleepily.

'It all made sense in the end. And it was something you said yourself Arabella that finally made me realize. It was when you said to Blackheart Jake that the Invisible One may or may not have been there, but that he *couldn't* see him. Then I realized that being invisible didn't have to mean that he was actually invisible – it just meant that people *couldn't* see him because they didn't know *how* to look. Then it seemed obvious to me that the most invisible person would likely be the one most in front of our eyes. Don't you see, the best place to hide is in the open…just as in the open square in front of everybody!'

Arabella and Michael let out an 'ahh' at the same time.

Ruu Eddin jumped up from his cushion. 'Exactly so! I am invisible, yet right in front of people's eyes, because nobody *sees* me. They don't know *how* to look.' He laughed and did a little jiggle in front of the others.

'Why is that?' asked Sophie when they had all stopped laughing.

Ruu Eddin sighed, 'Ah well, often it is judgment which stops people from truly seeing what is right before them. Judgment and expectations – they're both as bad as each other. And when people continue to live in judgment and expectation, then they will never truly fulfill their potentials.'

'Is that why this town is without color?' asked Michael.

'Exactly so. Exact-a-ly!' Ruu Eddin proceeded to play on an invisible flute which he made by putting his hands together and blowing. A delightful sound filled the air, the same as what Sophie and Michael had heard when in the factory room.

'That's a lovely sound,' commented Sophie. 'How do you make that without any instrument?'

'I do have an instrument!' said Ruu Eddin with a wink. 'Besides, it's one of my potentials. And here, it's very important to exercise and use our potentials. You wouldn't want to end up like those people here with their same-ish clothes and same-ish haircuts, now would you?' Everyone laughed, and Ruu Eddin continued to play wondrous music on his invisible flute.

'But what about all the people living in this colorless place...don't they see their problem?' Michael had been thoughtful about this for a while. Ruu Eddin stopped playing his flute and cocked his head to one side. 'I guess they don't, otherwise things wouldn't be as they are – would they? Such problems don't exist independently of you. They only exist here, in your head.' Ruu Eddin tapped his head and grinned. 'Your belief in such things is what makes them real. Potential is a question of perception - and some people only believe what they see, and see what they believe. But it's also more than that...'

Sophie, Michael, and Arabella were all listening intently to Ruu Eddin's words when suddenly he jumped up from his cushion and did a little dance and whirl while playing his imaginary flute. All the time beautiful, enchanting music flowed from his hands and filled the warm evening air of the colorful courtyard. If anyone had been spying on this little gathering they would have thought they were witnessing a scene out of the Arabian Nights.

'And what else…?' It was Arabella who finally broke the mesmerizing spectacle. Ruu Eddin stopped playing and bowed, playing the court jester.

'The truth, wherever it may be, is not only a question of perception - it is also a question of questions! You see, what's truly important for a person to be able to find the *invisible* is that they need to ask the right Question. What everyone is really searching for is the right Question - and yet we each already have this Question inside of us. It's just that we don't know how to find it because we aren't looking for it. You

cannot find something you're not looking for. So, first you must find

the Question inside of you, and then commit yourself totally to your

Question.'

'And the answer?' asked Michael.

Ruu Eddin shook his head. 'It's not about the answers. It never has

been…it's always about the questions. Find them first!' Then Ruu

Eddin continued to dance and play wondrous music on his special I-

can't-see-it flute.

The next morning they all gathered together over breakfast in the

colorful courtyard. That night each of them had slept, for the first

night in a long time, in soft, comfortable beds. Everyone had renewed

energies and high spirits. Sophie, Michael, and Arabella were all

laughing and joking together when Ruu Eddin entered and sat down

on his favorite cushion. A breakfast of cheese, olives, tomatoes, bread,

honey, with deliciously sweet tea, was all laid out on a bright colored

rug upon the floor. Everyone sat on cushions around the rug and ate in

contentment. Ruu Eddin seemed in an especially good mood, his

cheeky face lighting up with grins and winks. As always, he had draped over him his multi-colored robe, and his reddish-brown beard seemed more colorful and pointy-curly than normal.

'I can't believe that people just can't see you for who you are,' said Arabella as she munched on her honeyed toast.

Ruu Eddin smiled. 'Like you noticed me each day I came to visit you at the factory? You just thought I was an annoying idiot!' Ruu Eddin roared in laughter and everyone joined in - even Arabella who had a slight blush on her cheeks. He then turned to Sophie.

'But you, you picked up on something the first time you saw me in the square.'

Sophie nodded. 'I didn't know what it was at the time, but something wasn't right. I knew you had to be important to our search. You were there for a reason - and you are here for a reason now.'

Ruu Eddin pouted thoughtfully. 'Indeed, there is truth in what you say. I am here to get you here – first things first! Now you must be here too, in this present moment. No two moments are ever the same.'

'I remember the moment when you gave me the answer to my question that day. Do you remember what you said?' Sophie looked straight into Ruu Eddin's twinkling eyes.

'Of course.'

'You said that those who know the answer should share with those who don't know - and that you would not be needed and were going home!'

Ruu Eddin laughed. 'Yes, it was an answer to a fine question…though an obvious question which no one else had ever asked before. And you see, the answer told you how your world works. Your world is balanced out by those who know and those who don't.'

'And our search for No-Where? How do we get to No-Place?' interrupted Michael.

'Well, you can only get there by first arriving here. Yet no destination is an end in itself. Getting to No-Place may or may not get you to No-Where. There is no final end, there is only *further*.' Ruu Eddin gave them all one of his special winks.

'And how do we get further?' Arabella asked with a wink of her own.

'Now that,' replied Ruu Eddin with a raise of his hand, 'is the next step. Follow me!'

CHAPTER THIRTEEN – THE ROAD LESS TRAVELED

*When you know how to dream - really dream with strength and power
- you can achieve incredible things*

Sophie, Michael, and Arabella were standing outside the walls of the town, waiting for Ruu Eddin to appear. They had left the town by a back route, walking through the still colorless streets – unnoticed and seemingly invisible. Ruu Eddin had asked them to wait outside the walls whilst he went to fetch the transport. After all, they had to arrive at No-Place in style he insisted; and so they waited in anticipation. Finally, it seemed as if the road to No-Where was near at hand, and that they were closing in on their destination. The three youngsters were in high, energetic spirits until they saw Ruu Eddin arrive with the transport.

'Donkeys! You expect us to get to No-Where on a donkey?' Arabella was not well pleased, and was not afraid to show it either.

Ruu Eddin simply shrugged. 'What's expectation got to do with it? The donkey is the best form of transport for the road less traveled. It's also economical and you don't have to stop to fill it up with expensive liquid. What more do you need?'

Michael pointed at the donkeys, 'But there are only two of them – and we are four!'

'Exactly, exact-er-ly,' replied Ruu Eddin with a grin.

Arabella pouted, Michael frowned, whilst Sophie smiled, saying nothing.

The two donkeys were also loaded with bags of supplies hanging from their sides. Ruu Eddin took obvious delight in showing the proper way of mounting the donkey, and how two people were to ride together. It was *not* to the obvious delight of all.

On one donkey sat Ruu Eddin with Sophie behind him; on the other were Arabella and Michael. Both Sophie and Michael, as second passengers on the donkey, were not facing the front but were seated in reverse – facing the back of the donkey!

'Are you sure this is the proper way for two people to ride a donkey?' protested Michael.

Ruu Eddin wagged his head as he steered the donkey forward. 'Of course it is! The first rider has the view in front and the second rider keeps a view over the rear. This way we see what's coming and also what we're leaving behind.'

'Well, it just seems odd to me, that's all.' Michael looked over at Sophie who was likewise seated backward.

'It makes sense, if you don't think about it too much,' said Sophie as she playfully elbowed Ruu Eddin in his ribs.

'Yeowwh – here we go!' Ruu Eddin spurred the donkeys and they…slowly trotted off.

The walls of the colorless town faded into the distance as they left it behind. They eventually turned off the main road and followed a smaller lane that meandered through open meadows of the brightest colors. Trees, bushes, and flowers of different colors filled their senses and the day's gentle heat warmed their bodies. The first morning passed smoothly, with Ruu Eddin chatting away and telling stories and tales about his adventures which were, for the most part, quite unbelievable. The youngsters found the donkeys more comfortable than they had expected, and for Sophie and Michael – who were looking backward – the experience of seeing the path retreating behind them was rather satisfying.

SOPHIE'S SEARCH
FOR NO-WHERE

At mid-point during the day Ruu Eddin ordered a lunch stop, and spread a blanket on the floor which he filled with delicious specialties and treats. Traveling by donkey didn't seem so unfavorable after all. Also, the slower pace was a welcome change from the previous frenetic events and encounters each had experienced during their time in the Imaginal World. The slow donkey ride allowed each of them to reflect upon their own journey thus far. They were also feeling more relaxed than they had been in a long time. Under some shade by the lane the four friends enjoyed their tasty food.

'Are the Imaginal World and the Regular World really so different?' asked Sophie as she sipped her drink of sweet tea.

Ruu Eddin nodded, and then shook his head. 'Yes, and no – if you want to know the truth of it. They are different, of course. And yet they are so deeply connected, just like your left arm and your right arm. They do things differently, and yet they need each other. The Regular World always wants to try to fix things, to make them permanent. And so it clings to ideas and opinions, and doesn't want to let go of them. The Regular World can be quite stubborn like that. So what happens? The Regular World ends up turning the magical into stone, and things

become rigid. It can be so hard to move in the Regular World
sometimes. That's why those few of us here who could visit it, seldom
do visit. It just feels so *dense*!'

Saying this Ruu Eddin made stiff movements with his arms as if he
were a robot, which made everybody laugh.

'And then we have the Imaginal World here where things are fluid and
ever-changing. This allows more room for potentials to operate – yet it
also gives us more responsibility. Whatever we think or do here has
more effect elsewhere than we could possibly know. When you know
how to dream - I mean really dream with strength and power - you can
achieve incredible things.'

'Well, that's just what I don't get,' interrupted Arabella who had a piece
of cheese in her hand. 'Look, I know this food is delicious because I'm
eating it. And this cheese here must be the best cheese I've ever tasted.
And yet I know it's not real. I know we are all somehow in a shared
dream in this Imaginal World. So we're not really eating this food – we
only think we are. Right?

'Or maybe you're not really doing the things you do in the Regular
World – you only *think* you are. What's the difference?' Ruu Eddin
raised his hands and played a quick little tune on his now famous
invisible flute.

'Yeah, I knew I'd get a straight answer out of you,' muttered Arabella under her breath.

After lunch the four travelers continued along the winding lane until they came to a fork in the path.

'Which way now?' asked Arabella, who was facing forward on her donkey.

'I don't know, I can't see from back here!' called out Sophie.

'Me neither!' Michael tried to turn his head to see where they were.

'It's easy, no worries. When in doubt we always take the road less traveled. C'mon, follow on and further up.' Ruu Eddin steered his donkey down a narrow track that led away from the small lane. Every turn they made took them along an ever narrowing path. The one they were on now looked like it was seldom used.

'It doesn't look like many people use this track. Looks like it's used more by goats,' said Arabella after a short while.

'True, true. It's mostly a smuggler's track, but what better way to get to No-Place than through a smuggling route. After all, smugglers were the best at finding ways to No-Where!'

'Are you a smuggler, Ruu Eddin?'

Ruu Eddin turned back and grinned at Michael. 'Sure I am – it's what the Invisible One does best!'

As they were all laughing they didn't see two figures standing in the middle of the track ahead.

'Stop! This is a security checkpoint. No one passes here without being checked. Everyone off their donkeys!'

Ruu Eddin, Sophie, Arabella, and Michael all slowly climbed down from their donkeys and stood facing the two uniformed officers, Sergeant Spittlespat and PC Wobblekirk.

Sergeant Spittlespat came towards them and looked them up and down. 'What are you all doing here? Especially you, Ruu Eddin, what brings you down this smuggler's track?' Little drops of spittle flew from the sergeant's mouth as he spoke.

'Tell us, what brings you down this smuggler's track?' PC Wobblekirk wobbled slightly as he walked over to the group.

Ruu Eddin raised his hands and smiled innocently. 'Oh, well boys, I'm just taking my new friends here on a pleasant outing. I'm showing them the wonderful countryside we have around here.'

'And why take a smuggler's track?'

'Yes, why take a smuggler's track?' repeated PC Wobblekirk.

Ruu Eddin shrugged. 'It just seemed like the road less traveled – that's all!'

'Are you smuggling anything, Ruu Eddin? We've heard things about you and your antics.' Sergeant Spittlespat raised a suspicious eyebrow. 'Yeah, you and your antics.'

'Well, see for yourselves. There's just me and my friends, and our donkeys.' Ruu Eddin gave a coy smile.

'We will see for ourselves, indeed,' said Sergeant Spittlespat with a splattering of spit.

'Indeed!' added PC Wobblekirk with a wobble.

The two officers proceeded to search the bags strapped to the side of the donkeys. Yet after a thorough search all they found were provisions of food. Sergeant Spittlespat and PC Wobblekirk both scratched their heads.

'Well, in that case, can any of you tell us if you've seen Blackheart Jake? We've been after that scoundrel for donkey's years.' After he said that Sergeant Spittlespat looked apologetically at the donkeys. 'Ahem, no offence.'

'For my part, I have not,' said Ruu Eddin with a gentle bow. He looked over at the children.

'I haven't either,' said Arabella.

'Me neither,' added Michael.

'Nor me. But if you take my advice you should follow the silver cord inside of you. It will help to guide you. ' Sophie smiled at the two officers who both looked obviously bemused.

'Well,' grumbled Sergeant Spittlespat with flakes of airborne saliva, 'I guess you all should be making your way.'

'Yes, making your way,' echoed PC Wobblekirk.

The four travelers gave their thanks and mounted the donkeys once more and were off again.

'Good show back there,' called out Ruu Eddin. 'You know, its good etiquette not to tell the whereabouts of a person's goal. They have to find it themselves – otherwise they'd never appreciate it, and always blame you.'

'But are you a smuggler, Ruu Eddin?' asked Michael, half joking.

'Of course I am - amongst other things!'

'And are you smuggling things now?'

'Yup, I sure am!'

'And so what are you smuggling?'

'Donkeys!'

Ruu Eddin wiggled his fingers together and played another enchanting tune on his I-can't-see-it flute.

That evening the four of them made camp and enjoyed another delicious selection of foodstuffs from Ruu Eddin's seemingly endless supply. Each time Arabella put another piece of food in her mouth she knew it wasn't 'real' - but then again it tasted far better than any of the food she knew from back home. So which was the more real, she asked herself. Then again, the answer wasn't important…only the question was. That night they all slept under the stars, with blankets packed and brought by Ruu Eddin.

The following morning after breakfast the intrepid travelers once again mounted their donkeys and, seated in the same positions, continued along their journey. The narrow track soon reached a river and then ran parallel to the flow of the rushing water. After a short time they arrived at a rickety wooden bridge that crossed the river. Ruu Eddin decided that it might be too risky for both donkeys and their weights to cross the bridge at the same time. So Ruu Eddin, with Sophie seated behind him, steered his donkey onto the bridge first. The bridge creaked and rocked uneasily. Ruu Eddin's donkey cautiously made its way across, once or twice almost missing a step. Sophie, who was perched on the back facing in reverse, had the unfortunate view of seeing the faces of her friends on the riverbank as her donkey crossed the bridge. And the faces of her two friends were not reassuring. Neither was the sound of wood twisting and snapping. Sophie kept her mind still, telling herself that she needed to remain connected…that everything would work out fine. She had not come this far, so close to No-Place, to fail to reach No-Where now. Just as the rear legs of the donkey touched down upon the opposite riverbank then *whoosh* and the whole bridge collapsed into the river rapids and was swept away. There they were, with one donkey and two passengers on either side of the river.

'Ruu Eddin, what do we do now?' called out Arabella over the sound of the flowing water. 'And please, no more flute music!'

Ruu Eddin just lifted up his arms and shrugged. Then he sat cross-legged on the floor and closed his eyes.

Sophie sat down beside him. 'Are you sure this is the best thing we can do? Isn't there something more *active* we could be doing to help?'

When Ruu Eddin didn't reply Sophie decided to follow and she too closed her eyes. Everything fell silent except the sound of the water rushing by near their feet.

'Yeah, that's really not cool.' Arabella mumbled under her breath as she and Michael dismounted their donkey.

'At least they're safe,' added Michael.

'Safe, yes. Safely on the other side while we're stuck here with donkey genius.' The donkey hee-hawed and shuffled its feet bashfully as if it had heard.

'Something will come along, it always does,' said Michael reassuringly. Arabella let out a heavy sigh. 'That's exactly what I'm worried about. When something comes along here in the Imaginal World it usually spells trouble. I'd prefer *we* did something sooner rather than waiting for whatever-knows-what.'

'Maybe we'll meet some passing angels…' replied Michael somewhat sarcastically.

'Yeah, sure, maybe we will.' Arabella folded her arms and shook her head. Nice one, she thought.

No sooner had she thought that when there was a sound of voices in the distance. It sounded like a pair of men's voices chatting away. As Arabella and Michael looked ahead they saw two figures emerge from around a bend in the track, walking in their direction. Michael's eyes widened; he wasn't sure if he was seeing right. Then as the two men came further into view he knew his suspicions were right.

'I can't believe it – it's Ralph! And it's Gabby, too!'

Michael ran forward and Ralph greeted him with a big hug. Ralph was dressed in his familiar monk's robes and looked the same as when they had departed at the Monastery of the Sacred Blue Rose.

'Hey, it's my old pal Michael again. Fancy running into you along this way?' Ralph gave a jovial belly laugh.

Arabella ran to join them too. 'Fancy ain't the half of it. I know you Ralph, and there is no fancy coincidence about it, I'm sure.'

Ralph gave Arabella a big hug too. 'Hey, you're not still sore about getting lost in the Curving Canyons, are you?'

Arabella blushed slightly and gave Ralph a little punch on the arm. 'I paid for that by having to listen to all your tall monkish tales!'

Ralph again roared with laughter.

Gabby pulled a long face and shuffled his feet impatiently. 'Are we done with the loving reunion stuff? We've got to be somewhere, and sharpish soon. We can't forget what's written in the Scroll of Destiny. We've got a very important meeting to attend to.' Gabby took a paper scroll out from under his rags and unrolled it. He muttered to himself under his breath as he read it; his lips moving silently. 'Yep. We really need to get going, we haven't got much time left, and its real close.'

Gabby, lean and thin, was dressed in his customary rags, looking rather scrappy and destitute. He again was wearing his pair of white running shoes, which looked oddly out of place on the old man.

'Good to see you too,' said Michael, sticking out his hand for Gabby to shake. Gabby looked down at the young boy's hand and sighed. He reluctantly put out his hand for Michael to shake.

'How's the solar-powered buggy?' Michael asked enthusiastically. Gabby shrugged. 'I left it somewhere when it ran out of sun-juice. I'll find it later some day.'

Michael introduced his friend, and crazy buggy driver Gabby, to Arabella.

'Pleased to meet you, I'm sure. And it's great we have this reunion but, the thing is, can you two help us?' asked Arabella.

'Of course! What's the problem?' Ralph rubbed his hands together in anticipation.

Gabby coughed into his hand. 'Ahem, I'm sorry to spoil the party but we really must be going. The Scroll of Destiny says we need to be at an important gathering, and time is short. Maybe another time, kids.' Gabby quickly walked away and stood at the river's edge where the fallen wooden bridge had once been.

'Ah, don't mind my brother. He can be a real grump sometimes.'

'Your brother?! Both Michael and Arabella gave Ralph a look of surprise.

'Yeah, I know,' continued Ralph, 'we're so different. We're like wind and water sometimes. Well, he's the windy one!' Ralph laughed hard at his own joke.

Michael and Arabella looked around to see where Gabby was, and then they had another surprise. He was standing on the other side of the river – with their donkey! And he was chatting away with Ruu Eddin and Sophie.

'How did he do that?!' Arabella just stood there with her mouth open.

'Showing off again,' replied Ralph. 'Hey, bro, come back here! We have to help our friends.'

After several calls from Ralph, Gabby reluctantly agreed to come back across the river to their side. So he did – he just walked across the river as if it were normal ground. Michael and Arabella both blinked their eyes in disbelief.

'Did he just…?' stuttered Michael.

'Uh-hu,' muttered Arabella.

Gabby walked up to them briskly. 'Well, what's the problem? Come on, I haven't got all day.'

The children told Gabby and Ralph that they needed to get across the river to reach their friends on the other side. On hearing this Ralph laughed.

Gabby threw up his arms. 'Is that it? Why didn't you just say so in the beginning, instead of wasting our time? Come on.'

Gabby picked up Michael as if he were a feather and popped him on his back. Ralph likewise carried Arabella on this back, and together the two old guys walked across the river as if they were walking on dry land. When they got to the other side they put Michael and Arabella down, and reunited them with Ruu Eddin and Sophie. Ralph greeted Ruu Eddin as if they were old friends.

Gabby again coughed. 'Ahem, ladies and gentlemen, we really must be going. We don't want to be late for our gathering.'

'Why don't you and your brother come with us?' suggested Ruu Eddin with a broad smile. Ralph glanced over at Gabby with a questioning look.

'Noo, not going to happen I'm afraid,' replied Gabby shaking his head. And on this matter he was insistent.

The unlikely brothers Gabby and Ralph parted company and went on their way, with Ralph chatting cheerfully as he kept up with Gabby's brisk speed. Ruu Eddin, Sophie, Arabella, and Michael once again mounted their donkeys and continued onwards at their donkey-pace. Ruu Eddin informed them that they should reach No-Place by late afternoon. This news lifted everyone's mood and an energy of high spirits once again returned. Expectations were now running high amongst the three youngsters, even though they had been warned against this.

After a lunch that was enthusiastically eaten, and quickly, the three young travelers were eager to get back onto the donkeys. They could sense that their destination, and the end of their journey, was at hand.

And sure enough, after only a short time back on the donkeys, Ruu Eddin called out to the group.

'Around the next bend is No-Place! Are we ready, folks?'

'Yeah!' called out a chorus of young voices.

The two donkeys slowly ambled around the bend, and in front of them stood a...

...a small, grassy mound.

Everyone stared at the mound in front of them, yet no one said anything. It looked like a little belly bump upon the body of the Earth. There was a bubble of silence in the air.

Finally, it was Arabella who broke the silence. 'It doesn't look like much. It's just a little mound. Have we been searching all this time just for this?' Sophie and Michael were both peering around from where they were sat, on the rear of their donkeys.

Ruu Eddin shrugged. 'You can't blame me for your expectations – I did warn you all. Have you never seen a No-Place before?'

'She's right, it doesn't look like much,' added Michael.

'Is is really No-Place?' asked Sophie.

Ruu Eddin tutted. 'Of course it's No-Place – that's why it's so hard to find! It's the perfect place – who would ever suspect that here is No-Place? It can only be found by those who know what they're looking for. And that's why you need a guide. The Path requires a guide - otherwise you won't recognize a normal place from a No-Place.'

The two donkeys then trotted up onto the grassy mound until they had reached its centre.

'Ah, here we all are at last,' said Ruu Eddin with a satisfied smile. Then he drew his hands together and played a jaunty jingle on his I-can't-see-it flute. The three youngsters sat on their donkeys with confused expressions. Now that they had arrived at No-Place they had found…nothing.

'But there's nothing here…' murmured Michael softly.

'Have we journeyed all this way for no-thing?' whispered Arabella.

'Well, we've finally got to No-Place,' said Sophie scratching her chin.

'Now how do we find No-Where?

Ruu Eddin cleared his throat. 'Ah, yes – I forgot to mention…there is one more thing…'

CHAPTER FOURTEEN – THE QUESTION

*The people of the Regular World have a fixed destiny whilst those
of the Imaginal World receive that which is not in their destiny*

Everyone had dismounted and was now standing in the centre of the grassy mound. The three young travelers in the Imaginal World were waiting for Ruu Eddin to speak.

Ruu Eddin was pacing slowly around the mound, pretending to be absorbed in the grass and odd flowers that grew there. It seemed to Sophie, Michael, and Arabella that he was certainly testing their patience. Finally, after what seemed like too long a time, Ruu Eddin came over to where the three of them were standing together restlessly. 'It's true what they say,' he said. 'No-Where is only unreachable for those who believe they can't reach it. And you three have shown that not only do you believe that you can reach it, but also that you have the capacity to fulfill your journey. The final question is – what is *your* Question?'

The three youngsters looked at each other silently.

'Like I said before,' continued Ruu Eddin, 'everyone has a Question inside of them. Through this journey that each of you has undertaken

you should have arrived at your own Question. To know your
Question is the minimal price of admission to No-Where. You should
know that your travels in the Imaginal World were not solely to arrive
at No-Place, or any other physical place. It was so that you could arrive
at yourself – and to *your* Question. Each of you must now consider
this, and whisper your Question to me. The path to No-Where awaits
your Question…'

There was a long silence…a slight, gentle breeze wafted across the
mound; yet not a sound could be heard. Each of the three travelers had
retreated a moment into their own world – neither the Regular nor the
Imaginal World – and were searching for their connection, and for
their Question.

Sophie was the first to move. She stepped forward and walked up to
Ruu Eddin, who bent down so that his ear was close to Sophie's
mouth. Sophie cupped her hands and whispered something into his
ear. Ruu Eddin nodded, and Sophie stepped away. Then Michael came
forward and did the same. Only Arabella remained without the
Question, standing with her eyes closed. Several minutes passed and no

one said a word. It was a pivotal moment that would never come again for them – a moment which would determine the course of their lives. Slowly, Arabella opened her eyes and breathed deeply. She stepped towards Ruu Eddin who bent down to catch the flow of her whispered words – to catch the Question that was being let out from deep within her. Ruu Eddin nodded and Arabella stepped back to join Sophie and Michael.

Ruu Eddin nodded again and smiled. He looked each one of them squarely in the eyes with a look of approving grace. Silently, Ruu Eddin shared a blessing between them, and then he brought his hands together. For a final time he played an enchanting melody upon his invisible flute. A tingling vibration filled the air that made the hairs on the back of their necks stand up. The air around them also seemed to quiver, as if the air were like ripples upon an ocean. Then they appeared…

…they all stood before them upon the grassy mound. All smiling, some were waving, others clapping. Then together, in synchronization, they all gave a bow. There was Gali who waved; Ketav who was hugging her darling Starling; all the Huffalots jumping up together; Jimbob the Oldest Sproggit who was grinning and tipping his captain's hat; the Snifflegruffs Jedly and Fiffy looking excited; Eddie the Gangly was clapping with his strange human hands; Borik the Harkone was smiling broadly; Blackheart Jake was laughing and waving a vegetable rag doll in his hands; and Sergeant Spittlespat and PC Wobblekirk were giving the thumbs up. Even the terrible ghoul was there, looking cheerful and smiling, not looking half as bad as before. Then there was a flapping of wings and Sophie, Michael, and Arabella all looked up. In the sky overhead glided the majestic Lady Drakona. And she was not alone. With her were two winged figures, shining radiantly, and waving down from above.

Sophie gasped. 'It's Gabby and Ralph,' she mumbled softly. 'Actually,' said Ruu Eddin who was now standing beside her, 'its Gabriel and Raphael.'

Ruu Eddin stepped back and bowed. As if from nowhere another form suddenly appeared - it was the Green Man. The Green Man gave a slight nod of recognition to each of them - to Sophie, Michael, and Arabella.

'You have arrived at where you needed to be. You have each now succeeded in altering your own future. The people of the Regular World have a fixed destiny whilst those of the Imaginal World receive that which is not in their destiny.'

The Green Man reached out to his side and seemed to pull back the fabric of space. Or rather, he tore open a thin strip in the matrix of reality. From behind the gap another space shone through and beckoned.

'Welcome to No-Where,' he said. 'You may now step forward.'

SOPHIE'S SEARCH
FOR NO-WHERE

CHAPTER FIFTEEN – FINALLY...NO-WHERE

It is indeed a true power to have the strength to dream a new world into being

The sight was incredible – and totally unexpected. No-Where was anything but *nowhere*. The three intrepid travelers found themselves standing in a long hall with a high-vaulted ceiling, which stretched away in front of them. The walls of the hall were lined from floor to ceiling with books and files. The place looked like a vast library, with the bookshelves made of polished dark wood. The wood was so shiny it almost reflected the awed faces of Sophie, Michael, and Arabella. They walked through the hall slowly, each of them looking at particular books on the shelves. The names, they noticed, were rather strange. For instead of having names, like regular books, they had dates, strange markings, or just a small picture or diagram on the cover.

Sophie saw it first. It was a large golden plaque that was fixed to one of the bookshelves on the wall. It read

Destiny continues, but by no means abandon your own intentions, because if your plans coincide with the same direction then you will attain the fullness of what you truly long for within your heart.

SOPHIE'S SEARCH
FOR NO-WHERE

'Hey, look at this!' Sophie called over for Michael and Arabella to come and read the plaque. As all three of them stood there reading there was suddenly a noise that came from the other end of the hall. Somewhere a door opened and closed. They turned around to see a figure approaching them.

'Hello. Welcome to *The Hall of Records*. Yes, I know, it's not a very exciting name. Its other name, the one you're more familiar with, is No-Where – but that's even less exciting. You see, we aim not to arouse the false emotions too much here. Anyway, you can call here – that is, No-Where, whatever you want. After all, a name is just a name. Saying that, my name is Omar. And, again, welcome.'

The young boy who stood before them was thin, slightly dark skinned, and wore round, silver-rimmed glasses. His short, dark hair was neat and matched his tidy appearance. He couldn't have been much older than any one of them, maybe thirteen. He had a penetrating gaze, and yet his manner was gentle, confident, and reassuring.

'And why *are* we here?' asked Arabella in her typical no-nonsense fashion.

Omar gave only the briefest of subtle smiles. 'You are here because you followed your Calling. We all have this Calling, especially so when we are young, yet so few act upon it. And then it's too late - we become...adults.' This last word was said with a tinge of sadness.

'What's so wrong with that?' asked Sophie. 'I don't mind being an adult. We all have to be one day.'

'True.' Omar nodded his head thoughtfully. 'Then we will have other things to be getting on with. But for now, we have work to do in the Imaginal World. And no adults can enter into the Imaginal World.'

'Why is that? And why do we have to work?' Arabella wasn't sure she liked the idea of work – it sounded like it was something serious.

'Adults are not able to enter into the Imaginal World as their minds are already too closed and their sense of reality is too fixed. As for the work, well, it's something much more than that. Follow me.'

The three friends followed Omar down the hall, through a set of double swing doors, and down another corridor that was well lit despite there being no lights in sight. It all looked very normal. Michael could not stop himself from commenting on how normal it looked, as if he were back at school.

'That's the thing about the truly magical,' replied Omar, 'it can also seem so normal at the same time. Only the false magic stays fantastical because it's really a slight of hand trick, that's all!'

Omar led them into a fairly large circular room which had a table that dominated the centre. As they looked up they all noticed that the ceiling of the room was not a ceiling – it was a night sky full of stars, and colorful spirals, and whirling gas clusters.

'Well, some things can remain magical, of course.' Omar shrugged and allowed himself a smile.

'Is that the whole universe?' Sophie was enchanted with the view. She had always wanted to learn about astronomy and the stars.

'It's the universe that belongs to the SoA,' replied Omar.

'The SoA?' asked all three together.

'Yes, the Source of All. The Imaginal World comes from what you see out there. Here we experiment with forms, ideas, possibilities. Everything is so fluid here. We create from our minds, from our *intentions* - that's why we must be careful who comes here. The Imaginal World is not for everyone.' Omar pointed to the table in the centre of the room. 'Here, this is the table of the Directorate.' The large table was neither round nor square but had many sides.

SOPHIE'S SEARCH
FOR NO-WHERE

SOPHIE'S SEARCH
FOR NO-WHERE

Michael counted them. 'So there are eight of us in this...this Directorate?' It was an eight-sided octagonal table.

Omar nodded. 'I have been waiting to assemble my new team ever since I was appointed the Custodian of No-Where.' He made a slight shrug. 'As you can see, it doesn't sound like a grand title when you say it. Yet in this case No-Where is in fact better than somewhere. Things in the Imaginal World often function to the contrary, but not always – there's no rigid rules.' At this Omar gave a large smile. 'Anyway, we are now four, so we await four more others who are on their way as we speak. It is time to assemble a new Directorate'

'Who appointed *you* custodian?' interrupted Arabella.

'You really don't need to go there,' replied Omar with a slight raise of his eyebrows. 'Anyway, the Directorate will be eight of us, all exceptional in the fact that we made it here. Like I said, only us so-called "children" can cross over from the Regular World into the Imaginal World. Most of the people in the Regular World have no idea how it works. They just don't have a clue. And for most of them, its better they stay that way.'

'And how does it work, the Regular World I mean?' asked Sophie, now more curious than ever.

SOPHIE'S SEARCH
FOR NO-WHERE

'Let's sit down first.'

The four of them sat down at the octagonal table. It was made of a
material they had not encountered before – it was neither wood, nor
metal, nor plastic. And yet it seemed to give off a slight hum when
touched.

'We're all here,' began Omar, 'because we shared the same intuition.
The intuition that there was something not quite right about the
Regular World - that it wasn't all what we had been told. We all *felt* this
inside. This is what started us on our quest. And it's true – there is
something not quite right about the Regular World. In fact, there is
something very wrong with it. It's not going well.'

'What do you mean, it's not going well?' asked Michael.

'There have been too many destructive, and disruptive, thoughts
emanating from the Regular World. The people there are having so
many *bad thoughts*! And it's knocking the whole place out of balance. It's
been off course for a while. That's why it was decided that a
Directorate needed to be formed – from eight perceptive young people
who still had the power to dream.'

'Why the power to dream?' Sophie sat attentively in her seat.

SOPHIE'S SEARCH
FOR NO-WHERE

'Because it is through dreams that we can influence the Regular World. We can place specific ideas and images into people's minds while they are asleep. These thoughts, which then become their own, can help to steer the Regular World back on course. We can inspire people with new wishes, ideas – with new dreams for the future. You see, the Imaginal World contains many archetypes that already enter the Regular World in diluted forms. That's the way it's always been – it's how the Regular World exists.'

'Archetypes - what are archetypes?' asked Arabella.

'Archetypes are the principle ideas, or images, from which everything else is copied.'

'So the Regular World is a copy?'

'In a sense, yes. But it also has a life – a destiny – of its own. Yet sometimes it needs to be helped – it needs *to be steered.*'

Everyone fell silent after that. It was quite a statement to say that the Regular World – the world that each of the youngsters had grown up in and spent all their lives in – was in fact a copy.

Sophie leaned back in her chair, deep in thought. 'So,' she said finally, 'the Directorate is a group like us who help to maintain the reality of the Regular World, and who are responsible for its development and progress?'

'Exactly,' said Omar nodding. 'And the Directorate has to be made up of non-adults, like *us*, because we can still relate to that which is magical, sacred and special - that which is close to the Source of All. Only we are able to help filter some of this magical stuff down into the Regular World, not the adults.'

'The power to dream…wow!' remarked Arabella with an all-too-obvious grin. 'I always knew we children had something the adults didn't. Now I know for sure!'

'It is indeed a true power,' replied Omar. 'It is the power to be able to dream a new world into being. Dreaming has an important function in the Regular World. It is how the Imaginal World has always entered because it knows that what people dream will not only influence their life but the lives of others also. And that's why children's dreams are more important, don't you see? Children don't have the fear, the worries, the anger and hate that fill so many of the adult dreams. When such dark dreams escape and seep into the Regular World we have wars, destruction, and chaos. And then people begin to lose their hope, their grip on reality. A disease of despair and hopelessness can so easily infiltrate and poison the Regular World…and then…'

Omar's voice trailed off into silence.

'And then…what?' urged Michael.

'Then, sadly, the reality of the Regular World would collapse – and everyone with it. So, you see – we children *are* important!'

Later the three new members of the Directorate were alone at the table. Omar had left the room to attend to some matters, although it seemed as if he wished to give them some time on their own to think. Above them the stars, galaxy spirals, and colored clusters whirled with life that gave off a strange, hypnotic intensity. For a while no one spoke, as each was alone with their own whirl of thoughts.

Sophie was the first to speak. 'I know we are here for a reason. Remember what the Green Man said to us, before we entered here?'

'Yeah, he said something about the people of the Regular World having a fixed destiny, while those of us here in the Imaginal World somehow obtain that which is not in our destiny.' Michael looked across at Sophie and Arabella.

'We've been able to create something new. We've made decisions that have changed our lives - that's how we've been able to break away from a Regular World destiny. Now we're on a new path. And I think it starts here,' said Arabella, who was now in one of her more thoughtful moods.

Sophie nodded. 'Yes, it starts here. Everything is open before us. It's as if we've been released from a fixed destiny…'

'Released from the confines of the Regular World,' added Michael.

'Exactly,' continued Sophie. 'And with this freedom comes responsibility.'

'In dreams begin responsibilities,' said Arabella softly.

The whole room went quiet. It was as if each of them was thinking the same thing, and the sharing did not require words.

Omar returned to the room, reporting that another of the potential candidates for the Directorate had been spotted in the Imaginal World. He sat down with a wry smile on his face.

'Another one has just experienced the exile moment of the Snifflegruffs!'

They all laughed, especially Sophie. Then her face became more serious. 'This whole journey has been so much to process. I don't think I've yet fully taken it in.'

The others all agreed.

Omar nodded, also recognizing the sentiment. 'You will process it gradually over time, and the results of your understanding will emerge throughout your life in the Regular World. What you learn here you will also take back with you.'

'Are we to come and go as we please?' asked Michael.

'You live between both worlds now. As soon as you enter your dreams you will arrive here. If you agree, and we need your agreement on this, then for the rest of your life you – *we* – will be a part of the Imaginal World, just as we are a part of the Regular World. That's because every time you enter here you will be as a child again, despite your age in the Regular World. Time here, as you know, works differently. I'm somewhat older in the Regular World than I appear here.' And Omar gave a wink.

'And our time with the Directorate?'

Omar looked across at Arabella. 'That time will be limited. It must remain fluid, according to time, place, and people. There will always be a new group to come and continue the work. So it has always been, so it will always continue to be.'

Omar motioned for the group to follow him and he took them to another part of the complex, away from the Hall of Records. There he showed them incredible new things from the light of the stars that no words could ever describe.

Later, the group once more assembled in the Directorate room. Omar turned to the group and looked each one of them in the eyes. Then he gave the slightest of smiles.

'So, do you agree to join the Directorate - are you ready?'

CHAPTER SIXTEEN – IN A WORLD WHERE DREAMS FLOW

Everything is for a reason – everything connects

Sophie opened her eyes. She was lying in bed in her pajamas. A blue rose was attached to the collar of her pajama top. Sophie smiled, knowing just how deeply both worlds were connected.

It was morning, and she had to get ready for school. Downstairs at the breakfast table her father Richard was immersed in his tablet reading his morning emails, as always. Her brother James was munching on his cereals; his freckled face smirking mischievously as if he had just thought of a cunning, new plan. Her mother, Alice, was busy as usual getting everyone ready for the day ahead – her habitual duty. Everything seemed exactly the same, like every morning.

'Mum?' Sophie's voice was hesitant.

'Yes, Sophie – what is it?'

'How long have I been away?'

Her mother Alice paused and put the kettle down. 'Well, about eight and a half hours I would say…since you went to bed at eleven o'clock last night. Why?'

SOPHIE'S SEARCH
FOR NO-WHERE

Her father raised an eyebrow but did not look up from his tablet.

James giggled and stuffed himself with another mouthful of popping cereals.

'Oh, I just wondered,' muttered Sophie quietly.

'Did you go somewhere nice in your dreams, dear?'

Sophie looked up at her mother who was squeezing tea bags in their mugs.

'Yes, you could say that. I think I took the road less traveled.'

'That's nice, sweetie,' replied her mother.

'In dreams begin responsibilities…' said Sophie softly.

'Would you like some toast? And make sure that you'll be ready to leave for school shortly, won't you?

'Sure mum. No worries.'

SOPHIE'S SEARCH
FOR NO-WHERE

Sophie's day at school was the same as every other day. And yet it wasn't. After all, potential was a question of perception, as Sophie had remembered Ruu Eddin saying. And now Sophie's perception on the world – on the Regular World - was never going to be the same again. And not only was it a matter of perception; it was much more than that. It was a question of the Question that pulsated deep inside.

Later that evening when Sophie was sitting at her computer she received a friendship request on her social network page. It was from someone called Omar. He was, he said, getting the group together. Would she like to connect? Sophie knew it had begun.

Sophie knew, deep within her, that she was now a part of two worlds, and would remain so for all her days to come, and more. She felt lucky, and privileged, to be a part of this special journey. Inside her she had a connection that reached back, far back, to the Source of All. She knew that the future was going to last a very, very long time…and this gave her a warm feeling inside.

SOPHIE'S SEARCH
FOR NO-WHERE

You who are reading this — we are still waiting for the final candidates to arrive…

The Regular World needs you - the power to dream, to really dream, is now needed more than ever.

We are here now, speaking to you through these words. We know who is reading this book. We wrote it for you, to connect with you. Everything is for a reason — everything connects. We know what is going on in the Regular World, and it is time for change. You feel this too, don't you?

Are you ready for the power of dreams?